"Ping" | Elisa Munsó

ABSINTHE: World Literature in Translation is published twice a year by the Department of Comparative Literature at the University of Michigan.

ABSINTHE: World Literature in Translation receives the generous support of the following schools, offices and programs at the University of Michigan: Rackham Graduate School, Office of the Vice Provost for Global and Engaged Education, International Institute, and the Department of Romance Languages and Literatures.

Typesetting and Design
William Kalvin, Delmas Typesetting. Ann Arbor, Michigan
delmastype.com

Printed at McNaughton & Gunn. Saline, Michigan
ISBN: 978-1-60785-514-9
ISSN: 1543-8449

sites.lsa.umich.edu/absinthe
Follow us on Twitter: @AbsintheJournal

ABSINTHE: A Journal of World Literature in Translation

DWAYNE HAYES	FOUNDING EDITOR
SILKE-MARIA WEINECK	EDITOR-IN-CHIEF
YOPIE PRINS	CHAIR OF COMPARATIVE LITERATURE *at* THE UNIVERSITY OF MICHIGAN—PUBLISHER
JUDITH GRAY	ADMINISTRATOR
ELIZABETH FERTIG GRAHAM LIDDELL GENTA NISHKU	MANAGING EDITORS

ABSINTHE

WORLD LITERATURE IN TRANSLATION

*BARINGS // BEARINGS: CONTEMPORARY
WOMEN'S WRITING IN CATALAN*

ABSINTHE 25 | SPRING 2019

A selection by Megan Berkobien and María Cristina Hall

ABSINTHE 25   TABLE OF CONTENTS

FROM THE EDITORS:

Over forty years ago, in the midst of the democratic transition following the death of dictator Francisco Franco, author and activist Montserrat Roig contemplated her duties as an *"ésser civic"* in a moment of intense cultural and political change:

> Escriure en català és una afirmació de supervivència, i no solament literària. Ganes "d'existir" privadament i col·lectivament [. . .] Si tot va bé, escriure en català ja no serà un acte de "salvació" sinó un acte natural, un acte intern i privat que dóna coherència als sentiments i a les frustracions personals.

> [To write in Catalan is an affirmation of survival—and not just in literature. A will "to exist" privately and collectively [. . .] If everything works out, writing in Catalan will no longer constitute an act of "salvation," but a natural endeavor, an internal and private act that makes sense of our feelings and personal frustrations.]

For years, communicating in Catalan was an act of witnessing—of lending testimony to an ever-precarious past and present. While this understanding of Catalan as resistance is necessary, Roig contends that mere survival has never—will never—be enough. Instead, a language of the living should reflect the *feeling* of its people. And perhaps it's no surprise that this kind of writing is typically coded as feminine.

While our political and cultural context is decades and miles different from Roig's, our work, too, was born out of desire: to render visible the many labors of contemporary women writing in Catalan, and that of the many translators who craft their stories into English. Many of the texts here highlight and grapple with emotional labor and other responsibilities traditionally assigned to women, and what connects the struggle presented by Roig and our own is the labor of our craft: translation as a way to keep our worlds vital, empathetic, and expressive—a rewarding yet woefully unrecognized toil.

In several ways, *Barings // Bearings* is a response to another remarkable anthology titled *Women Writers in Catalan*, which was put out recently by the Catalan publishing house Raig Verd. A sharp response to a cultural context still dominated by male writers, it comes as no surprise that the anthology's editors were duly concerned with visibility, as captured in the common refrain at the release party: "Celebrem que existim!" ("We celebrate our existence!"). Yet, most of the excerpts appear in English by way of a handful of hired translators, who, by no fault of their own, remained largely unaware of the many translators who were already undertaking the endeavor. In many ways, this volume of *Absinthe* is a site for these fabulous translators to make clear that they exist, too, giving them the chance to break into the competitive world of literary translation.

Barings // Bearings is a testament to the thriving worlds of women's writing in Catalan, with time-travelling fiction by Bel Olid (tr. Bethan Cunningham), regrets on pregnancy sublimated into an airborne taxi ride in a story by Tina Vallès (tr. Jennifer Arnold), Mireia Vidal-Conte's poetry reflecting on Virginia Woolf's suicide (tr. María Cristina Hall), a story of revenge on an abusive elderly woman by Anna Maria Villalonga (tr. Natasha Tanna), as well as reflections on war, bookstores, and generational conflict in post-Franco Spain. These often surreal pieces of Catalan fiction are informed by several essays and works of literary memoir, including those by Marta Rojals (tr. Alicia Meier) on the state of the Catalan language and Najat El Hachmi (tr. Julia Sanches) on the conditions of growing up in Catalonia as the daughter of Moroccan parents. These latter pieces resist and explore the contours of multilingualism, highlighting the intra- and interlingual reality of spoken Catalan alongside Spanish and Amazigh.

For the early-career translators in this issue, this publication follows years of immersion in Catalan culture, countless hours honing our translation skills, and much solidarity. We only hope this issue will highlight and commend the important work these writers and translators are building today. So give yourself over to feeling, for, as Montserrat Roig reminds us: "La cultura és l'opció política més revolucionària a llarg termini," or, "In the long run, culture is our most revolutionary political option."

Megan Berkobien & María Cristina Hall

"Top on the Red Mountain" | Elisa Munsó

NAJAT EL HACHMI

From *I Am Also Catalan*

(literary memoir)

Translated by Julia Sanches

Lately, immigration is regularly discussed: in the media, on the street, at any terrace gathering. . . . People speak of inflatable dinghies, illegals, church closures, deportations, expulsions, integration and fundamentalism, among other things. Research on the subject is abundant; how many have arrived and how many stayed, what they do, the quality of their Catalan, numbers and more numbers that try to make sense of a new reality as incomprehensible to most as it is unfamiliar—a reality that's feared even, and often distant.

* * *

"Mom, what's that, huh? What is it?" you ask me from your ninety-seven centimeters of bustling curiosity, your eyes wide open. You don't pay close attention to my response, maybe it was a rhetorical question. Your interest shifts to the television, muted by the sounds of the washing machine. You get closer and start yelling: "I like water!" When a commercial is really good, you can tell from the first few notes and you run to it like a mouse after the Pied Piper. A few seconds later you're kneeling at the rug, without knowing that your mother had put it in the dining room because she missed the feeling of sitting on the ground and resting her head on the cushioned walls. You don't know that world, not yet, and when you do, eventually, it might seem a bit alien. You grab your foot and rock back and forth while trying out different points of view, watching the screen upside down. We've all done it at some point, suddenly everyone's bottom-up. You tumble clumsily a couple of times then search in one of your secret hiding places for a tiny, tiny car, the kind that comes in chocolate eggs. You assume your original position. After observing your foot for a moment, you stare at your fingers and yell, outraged:

"Look, mama, I have *axan!*"

You don't mix the two languages so much anymore, but there are words you always say in Amazigh; even though you know the word for nails, you enjoy saying *axan* instead. Maybe because I've always spoken to you as if you were my travel companion, from the very first day, from the moment they placed you on my chest, your head slightly dented from your passage through the vaginal canal. A mother learns to codify her child's language. I won't insist on explaining that everyone has nails and that what you're trying to say is yours have grown. I know that with your persistent hardheadedness you'd spend a good while arguing the opposite. I suppose your language has its own logic, one no one else can understand. Even though you always elect to speak in Catalan, I'm certain your linguistic code must be an amalgam of this language and the one that once, a long time ago, was your mother's mother tongue.

Before you were born, even far before you were even conceived, your dad and I decided we'd speak to you in Amazigh. Not out of any sort of patriotic fervor, no, but so you could have another tool at your disposal to interpret the world. Not giving you the opportunity to learn the language of your ancestors would have been criminal to your upbringing and to the increasingly feeble ties that bound you to Morocco. The place of your father's grandparents, your aunts and uncles, your cousins, eight years of your mother's past and about twenty of your father's, not to mention, of course, the sporadic holidays, a ten to fifteen-day escapade, and phone calls with a very distant *hanna*. You listened carefully, and with some shock, to your father as he explained to you that this woman was his mother. Maybe you were surprised one person could be called both mama and iaia—mom and grandma—maybe all you express in the face of the many new things you learn is this innocent surprise; everything becomes a miracle to your eyes framed in curled lashes.

For the first couple of years, we managed to stick to our plan. We'd often see Moroccan kids speaking only in Catalan or Spanish and feel a little embarrassed for those parents who weren't properly educating their children. We always judge others blindly until we find ourselves in a similar situation and have to recalibrate. I remember making you a part of my neurosis when you were only a few days old, explaining to you, full of hope, the story that was taking shape, delivering a sarcastic critique of the nonsense we'd both watch on TV, or a detailed account of current international affairs. You were one of the best interlocutors I'd ever met, listening without interruption, sometimes wrinkling your nose or half-smiling in disapproval, and you knew how to keep a secret. Now that you can speak, I can't do that anymore. A few months ago, it occurred to me to explain that we were on our way to the doctor so they could have a look at your penis, and how embarrassed was I when you started yelling on the street: "We're going to the doctor to look at my penis! We're going to the doctor to look at my penis!" Maybe I should have started by explaining what privacy is—but how?

⁂ ⁂ ⁂

Ours is a beautiful love story, we've spent more waking nights together than all the lovers of literature across the universe; none of them would've weathered the trials of your first four months of life. What did it matter that I was sleepy, if you were hungry? Who said four in the morning isn't just the perfect time to demand entertainment or start wagging your tongue? Some nights, already exhausted, the bags under my eyes reaching the floor, after waking your dad, you ceaselessly crying in my arms and me not understanding what exactly you wanted, I thought that maybe a few years later I'd laugh it all off. And so I did, now that you're just shy of three and eating all on your own, going to the bathroom all on your own, and expressing clearly what's hurting or bothering you, it all seems so far away and I can't help but smile when I think of it.

How will you express yourself this Christmas, when we go away? Last time we were there, you hadn't even turned one, and with enormous effort you'd blabber on in a strange language no one could understand. In the beginning, every word uttered by your little mouth was in Amazigh, you even called me *iimma*, though it's been a long time now since you've started calling me mama, or even mami. *Iimma* meant seeing myself reflected in your eyes in my mother's likeness, and something deep inside me would move. Mama is much more neutral, the figure of a mother that is unknown to me, one I've never encountered from up close.

The big change came in nursery school—you were so frightened those first few days! Soon, though, you became used to that new universe and, I guess, must have caught onto the admiration I felt every time you said a new word in Catalan. I was scared you wouldn't be understood, you'd always been so chatty, but then your teacher told me time and again that you hadn't breathed a word. I still can't believe you spoke so well after only two months, but that's how it went and nowadays no one can pry a word of Amazigh out of you.

You fall asleep on the floor, just like you've always liked. Where does this habit come from? You kneel and start rocking all on your own, singing until sleep gets the better of you. Maybe you know that your mother, and all your ancestors, slept on the floor as children. I doubt it, but customs also live on in our genes; they're part of your genetic legacy.

Like that, with your eyes closed, your long lashes casting shadows onto your rosy cheeks, anyone might say you'd never broken a single plate—after an entire day of emptying out your closet, unmaking my bed, of dragging along the cushion as if it were a horse, smearing your entire head with that expensive cream I hadn't even had a chance to crack open. . . . And there are days when you're exhausting, but I wouldn't take it back, not for anything. In fact, seeing you grow so fast is a little like facing the abyss of tomorrow, I don't even want to picture the day you leave home. There's still a while to go, but sooner or later all things come to pass.

* * *

Right in the middle of this cloister of age-old columns you lean into the pond surrounded by greenery; belly-down, legs stretched out all the way, your hands gripping the edge and almost brushing the water, you contemplate the brilliance of the red fish that swim seemingly unaware of your presence, utterly enchanted. You don't dare plunge your fingers into the water since by now you've heard me say "no" a few times. You look at me for a moment and, happy to be there, in that place, ask me.

"Oi, this is my *virsititat*, isn't it mama, isn't it?"

"Yes, Rida, yes, this is your university."

Possessiveness must also be a thing quite of this age. I think that for you a university is no more than that pool of water full of wondrous animals, circled by a strange building, who cares if it's the School of Philosophy or Mathematics. It's because of this that every time I need to check grades or run an errand, I try and bring you with me. When the time comes to leave, the great spectacle of crying ensues, with tears and extortionate hugs so I'll let you stay just a little while longer.

Back when you'd only just started kicking in my belly, enveloped in amniotic fluid, we were already walking together through the classroom; between dizzy spells, we would settle as best we could onto those old and narrow wooden benches which, of course, hadn't been made with pregnant women in mind.

In this corner of the world, with the muffled roar of traffic outside (I'd never get used to living in Barcelona, there was so much noise, so much hurrying, it was madness), a mother ceases to be mother, wife, daughter, worker, house mistress, immigrant, Moroccan, Berber, or Amazigh. A mother, my son, sheds all labels and is only herself. Sometimes, transported by the effort to understand some concept or entranced by a new discovery, a new word or a new author, she even sheds her own body and, in that moment, becomes only thought. This impulse is what made me keep studying, taking the train each day, an hour and a half there, an hour and twenty back, missing you on days when I barely saw you, with so many things to organize so that I could find a moment to study, to read. A little selfish, maybe, I know, but at the end of the day, you seem to understand that mom is happier now that she's back in class. I don't think my postpartum depression was exactly that, but rather a depression caused by the fact that it was the first time in my life I didn't have to take notes or prepare for exams, a symptom of abstinence perhaps. Luckily, in just six months I'd already signed up for English classes, which must have been my methadone, a proxy of three to four hours a week.

Hasiba, Khadija, Faisal, Fàtima, Najat. . . . Who could have known we'd all followed parallel paths and finally meet at university. We'd all arrived here at the age of eight or nine, some earlier, had grown up in a country that wasn't ours and, at first, experienced the same contradictions, the same uncertainties, and missed a part of ourselves, the one we'd left behind in Morocco. Now, we will rule among the chrestomathies of Emilio García Gómez, poetry for the ignorant, the greedy of Khorasan and lost kingdoms in order to recover that parcel of ourselves that came loose at some point along our path that was neither first or second generation.

And you, son? Will you search among the stones of this ancient building for something to fill the vacuum left by your upbringing in this educational system? Will you want to learn Arabic, even by dint of dictionaries and irregular roots? At the end of the day, Arabic is not only your parents' language but the language of oppressors in a land where the Amazigh were considered second class; language that's only oral; barbarians, they called us. Will you feel hurt the day you return to Morocco and are spoken to by those in power in the language of the prophet, of the king? They'll probably scorn our sounds, but this won't feel unfamiliar to you. Your other mother tongue, Catalan, was in another time also scorned and misunderstood, and it isn't for nothing that your mother considers them sister languages.

I hope that sooner or later you'll realize that the amalgam of linguistic codes you're growing up with can only be enriching. I hope that, like your mom, you'll learn to love each language equally; as historic patrimonies, the oldest legacies of every civilization, music that comes to us from very far and which we must strive to preserve. You'll know there is no language or dialect better or worse than another—they all serve to express our feelings and desires, our frustrations.

ANNA PANTINAT

From *Suddenly a Summer*

(poetry)

Translated by Gabriella Martin

La Conca

Buoyed by my seashore, a stripped-down crew on this rocky whale, endearing every day. I will play along to belong, yes, I will. And with the same baskets and matching sandals, we'll call ourselves a community without shame. We'll sail, carried away by the wind and the current, to become, little by little, brazen, liminal, isolated, barbaric.

ARTEMIS

Nocturnal as the logs
stacked in the cellar,
the hunter is still.
Cat's eyes, breathing to the beat
of her prey, synchrony
of a precise motion, the chance
has come.

The present so multiplied,
set to flames in this fraction.
Right here.
All alone.
Now.

"And, scattering the aligned letters,
my soul saddens
remembering the snow drifts sullied
by tourists' dirty footprints."
VÍCTOR RAHOLA

Notes

My first friendships are the truest. Workers, summer vacationers, towns-folk. With the second generation comes Risk, tarot cards, Anaïs Nin, Eva, lipstick on cigarettes, an exploding empty glass.

Elysian

The other world is here, it still is:
the fluid medium of phantoms
slicing wind gusts like shovels through smoke.

The visible ones and the bodiless legacy,
glistening skins swimming gently, unceasing.
Social life and the other life.

Maritime Arrangement

The fabrics arrive by boat from India, bought on credit. I'll sell them at an outrageous price. "It's Empordà." I don't have a room of my own here, but I work in a shop with a view.

Scuba Diving

It was a difficult choice. So many waves and so many books muddle one's sense of transcendence, this tiny rowboat of a well-turned phrase.

"Pájaros en la cabeza" | Elisa Munsó

ESPERANÇA CAMPS

"Birds"

(fiction)

Translated by Katherine Reynolds

I killed her, your Honor. I wasn't desperate. I couldn't even say I was crazy about her. She was beautiful, yeah, attractive, but she wasn't the only girl in the world. I wasn't desperate. I saw her every day at the factory. The office was above the central part of the warehouse and from there we can see the entire production process. The damned workers can't see us but we keep an eye on every move they make. If they talk, if they pick their nose, or if they scratch their balls. We know how much time each worker wastes during the day. From up there, your Honor, we can see right down the women's tops. It can get up to 95 degrees in the warehouse you know? Damn hot and damn horrible. Installing air conditioning would be really expensive and counterproductive for the products we manufacture, which need to be kept at a constant temperature and the boss says that air conditioning the factory doesn't matter, and this way we get to enjoy the view of all that flesh on display all year round. To me that seems cruel, right? Pretty shitty thing to do. But you get used to it easily. My table's next to the window and I hardly have to lift my head and I have the full panorama right in my eyeline. I can take my pick. But I didn't choose, you understand? My eyes always went to the same girl. To the one in charge of packaging. She was right at the end of the production line. There's actually four of them who do it but my eyes always went to the same one. I couldn't help it, your Honor, I couldn't, I couldn't, no . . . I didn't even raise my head, all I needed was a slight movement and I had her right there in front of me: ripe, sweaty, tanned, exhausted. I had her right there: ripe, sticky, beads of sweat trickling down her face, along her neck, and pooling between her breasts. The machinery stopped me from seeing her whole body but the sweat and the cleavage and her black curls were enough. She wore a very thin gold chain around her neck. Little gold, little money. I don't like gold myself. Poor people wear it to seem like they're a bit richer than they are. Twice I tried to bump into her at the factory entrance. The managers have a separate entrance but sometimes, so we don't seem mean or affected, we go in through their door. They say hello to us, practically worship us. The majority of them are immigrants and they don't always have the right paperwork, you get my drift, what with the way things are you can't be quite so strict and if there's a stamp or a visa missing, well you can bring it to me later and start when you like. It also makes it easier for us to get rid of them without having to explain why. We have to do these little tricks because of production. If we want to stay in business, the competition's really tough, your Honor, and the Chinese make it really difficult for us, you know this already, it's in the papers every day, and about how we need to revive manufacturing. . . . Yes, you asked me why I killed her and I've still not told you, it's because I don't really know. A couple of times I made sure I ended up walking alongside her when we clocked in. I greeted her nicely, yes, I was really friendly, I said to her, hello, how are you? And she just looked at me. She didn't say anything to me. Hello how are you? It's not offensive, your Honor. She didn't say anything. She just looked at me. And the next day as well. A greeting, and silence. Two silences are a lot, your Honor, because I watched her from above. I knew every drop of sweat that glistened on her body and if I said good morning to her, she had to say good morning to me. So one morning, I took advantage of the boss being out in meetings, I called her on the tannoy and made her come up. She jumped when she heard her name on the speakers. The other workers stared at her. You should have seen her; she was shaking like a leaf. From fear and cold. In the office we do have air conditioning and we turn it right up. The beads of sweat froze on her face and neck. Why don't you answer when I say good morning to you? Why don't you look at me? And she just kept her eyes fixed on the floor. Look at me. And she lifted her head with a yes sir which wasn't right for her, your Honor, like this, look, she lifted her head like this and she looked daggers at me and said what do you want, in a firm, powerful, warm, even voice, and she was looking at me and I was speechless. She couldn't have that voice, your Honor. Not that voice, do you understand what I mean? That woman had a voice that hurt me. How did I not know it? And because I wasn't answering she was insisting, what do you want sir, my friends are having to cover for me and I wouldn't want them to be angry. And she kept on talking, vocalizing, spitting birds from her mouth, vomiting a mortal melody while saying she was in a hurry. I was no longer paralyzed, she'd got me going, your Honor. I was turned on and the air conditioning wasn't enough for me, that right there, facing the false window I went towards her and in one quick blow to her back I pulled her towards me and the phone rang and the answerphone kicked in and she resisted and I was already kissing her because I was superior, I was stronger, I was a man on fire, me, your Honor, it was her fucking voice that got me there, so much fucking melody just to say what do you want sir, I've got work to do, and I was touching her breasts, which were frozen, pearly with cold sweat and I wasn't able to stop and if you want, your Honor, I won't finish telling you all the details which I think are already in the indictment and I don't know if now's the right moment to tell you the rest, here in front of the members of the jury, 'cause there are ladies here who could be offended, because a man, when he's turned on he does things that afterwards are ugly to describe. She resisted and I couldn't stop myself and when her shift finished her bewildered co-workers looked up at the office trying to see why she hadn't come down but they went without waiting for her although they didn't know she sat dead in my office chair. And she shut up but I still saw how the birds that flew from her mouth got tangled up in her black curls.

MIREIA CALAFELL

Selected Poems

(poetry)

Translated by Adrian Nathan West

Barcelona

I recall that cruel pain in the retinas
the eve when, of a sudden, we saw so much clearer.
It was a coincidence, inexplicable:
first we heard the *cheese* of a half-million voices
then the camera flashes came in bursts.
How the light hurt, that light so white
it left no shadows, it lit up all under its rays:
how the people shouted facing the barrage.
Afterward, clairvoyance: we learned the truth
of this city of ours made for the others,
we dug up nails at the feet of buildings,
blocks of cardboard blocks of wood, open pails of paint
and other materials for modern, cosmopolitan décor.
I remember your shudder and the question's tone:
if it's all a farce, are you and I just extras?
And I looked then as now without knowing what to tell you,
and we walked off in silence, hand in hand
like lovers printed on a postcard.

For Maite Lafarga

The whole year long, a galling wait
for a trilogy: sea, salt, and you.
Then the miracle ensues and August comes
—as it came the summer before.
This year, though, the sand engulfs you
and doing like the rest is impossible:
you can't make for the wave
and plunge into the joy of the beach
for nothing in the world will you deny what you now know,
not just salt, but ashes are floating in the water.
Not you. You will not forget your mother.

Guileless whales

What joy the play of the whales
when there were no species or hemispheres.
What complicity beneath the sea
before the rift, the stampede,
the elusion without knowing why
to other oceans, and separating,
the inexplicable splitting of the ice.
And never again the timeless days
when all there was to do was leap,
and waves were no longer gifts
but rather mementoes of distances,
the enduring pain of having lost another.

They love, I know they love.
It's easy to see it in their eyes,
the tectonic movement of valediction,
the anguish in the beasts' gaze,
how high you and I leapt.

Certainty

Knowing how to interpret the words
of an empty pool amid the cold,
a Ferris wheel stalled on a humdrum Monday
sans sugar clouds or neon lights,
or a circus tent dismounted
—enough of acrobatics, trickery, magic.

Understanding and accepting that they are also this:
tedious days, devoid of attraction,
an eerie landscape that harbors menace,
that makes itself present cyclically.

Knowing this is, at the same time,
accepting the certainty that your body
will not be—cannot be—every night
this present holiday.

"Two Flowers" | Elisa Munsó

LOLITA BOSCH

From *What You're Seeing Is a Face*

(fiction)

Translated by Nathan Douglas

And I continue:

Like every other day in your life before, you open the windows
and look toward the street outside. You focus. Apart from what is out
there, though, you can't quite make out anything else. You never see
anything else. And, even if you don't remember it, you think that someday, someday, you will finally stumble upon something that makes you
understand that the street is nothing more than a gray line, asphalt, and
you've always wondered just how far it would take you if you followed it,
though you never have. Even if you don't remember it, that's what you
think about today while you close the window, because now you know
that what caused you to open it in the first place is no longer interest-
ing, and whatever you might see out there doesn't matter anymore once
you focus on it, and you fumble for a cigarette in the dark as you recall
restless nights of sleep, but the night doesn't bother you anymore and
you find a cigarette with no filter, half smoked, you light it up in a hurry,
nearly burning your fingers in the process, a pain that, for a second,
tempts you. But you're never embarrassed because nobody will ever find
out, and nobody will ever know that you're thinking about what might
happen if you burned your hand, if you made a little hole right in the
center, a stigma, and despite you knowing very well that that would
never ever happen, you can't stop thinking about it, because you want to
know, despite no one telling you otherwise, if it's even remotely possible
for something that's completely out of your control to happen. And right
when you're on the verge of burning your own hand just to see what'll
happen, you convince yourself—definitively, once and for all—that
you can't do it because it's just never going to happen, kind of like the
things that would happen tomorrow if only someone would realize they
were happening, but either way you'd invent some believable excuse
and since you know that everyone would believe it you decide not to
do the wrong thing, but the right thing, because it was too risky a move,
anyway: they'll always want to believe whatever you say, but the truth
burns. So you put the cigarette out, you flop back onto your bed, you
stop breathing just to feel dead for a little bit, and you try to see yourself
through the glass lid of your casket, but you can never quite recognize
your own breathless lips, and while all this is happening the sun comes
up and you feel anxious because you aren't sure you've even slept at all
and then from someplace there's a voice *you don't look so well* and then *I
don't even remember sleeping* and now who knows if you wanted to burn

yourself in the first place. But nobody will ever know, and only now do you understand that. And you look for another cigarette, you light it, and you go to the kitchen to make yourself coffee thinking that you would love yourself more if you didn't have to say hello to anyone, because you feel an uncomfortable coldness that for some reason you seem to think only absence can warm up, though you're certain absence doesn't exist or, if it does exist, you—specifically you—are incapable of recognizing it because you only look for ways around it but never come to any real solution, convinced that, given the way you are, solutions don't matter, just knowing you'd be capable of thinking of one is enough. And you know, you know for sure, that today you will still be incapable of it because you can already hear those annoying neighbors of yours, and you're not sure why today, today again, again like every other day but especially today, they're making noise so early. Again.

When you were young nothing scared you more than thinking about war before you went to sleep, but that didn't stop you from making a habit of it, you imagined scenes, fearfully dramatic visions like the ones you see now, the silhouette of your mother wandering along the street in search of a bomb shelter or your sister begging for food, your house destroyed, your dog dead, photographs, books, your diary, toys . . . everything burned, and your helpless brother crying among the ashes. But you only imagined such things when your father took you to sleep over at your grandmother's house. Only in that strange room paneled with the same kind of wood as the houses for pet birds that they sell at the supermarket, with two beds—immobile—nailed to the ground, the nightstand, the closet full of hand-painted hangers that you always want- ed to steal, the painting of a ship tossed about on a ruthless, angry sea, the window that stayed permanently hidden behind those heavy black cur- tains whose fabric fell in a forceful cascade to the floor, and that wooden figure of Christ whose face grimaced with all the pain in the world, your sister sleeping in the other bed while you would lie paralyzed by insom- nia in yours, you couldn't do anything and you knew it, and I don't know why you ever thought about wanting to turn your bed into a sea and your body into a boat, devouring the bodies of all those sailors like the body of Christ in order to cure your insomnia as if restlessness were as beguiling then as it is now, but just as it doesn't matter now, it wasn't important then, since it was all a trick and you were already in the habit of lying, so you'd try the window again and when you realized you couldn't see anything outside of it, you'd imagine a war instead. This you know for sure: you know that you will never explain those made-up wars to anybody and how when you spent the summer away from that house you could forget them or at least that's what you thought and you didn't want to die like that until the next summer came, but today, just today, precisely today, this exact day, on today's date, you remember all of this as you put out your cigarette and make your way to the bathroom, thinking almost instantly once you've looked in the mirror without recognizing yourself that nobody can really remember who they are after surviving a war and as you pull back the shower curtain to run a bath you think for a second that you see three piles lying in the tub: one with your hair another with your shoes and the third one empty because you don't have any gold teeth but that doesn't stop you from sweeping a couple of fingers around your mouth to make sure all of the pieces are where they should be. Here they are: child's teeth of pure ivory you brush in the time it takes the tub to fill with scalding water and after it's done and begins to cool you go to the kitchen to pour yourself a coffee and you wish that today nobody had woken up but the neighbors keep making noise though you don't ever plan on saying anything to them and you sit down on the sofa to drink your coffee one small gulp at a time until you suddenly stop to look at your hands and are surprised to see a mark in the middle of one of them you had never noticed before. You don't know when you burned your hand and I myself can't recall either, I only know that if it were cold you could put on some mittens to hide it but it's hot so you decide to ignore the wound when the telephone rings, you decide not to answer but that doesn't stop you from getting up from the sofa to turn down the volume on the answering machine and sitting back down for more coffee. And just today, this draining and unending day, you don't want to do anything or see anyone or even go outside and it's evident too that you don't want to know where that gray line of asphalt leads and there's only one way to avoid it, the same way as always, the way that's impossible to ever really make happen now that you're constantly resorting to it: the same, the only distraction you invent and reinvent over and over again is to find explanations, urgent excuses you abuse just for the sake of not moving, perhaps in order to try to understand why you suddenly feel panic, real panic, not some urge to talk about life or some daring impulse to once and for all confess all of your fears to the nurse and finally make everyone else understand that today you are a person who needs nothing more than blind comfort, some sort of unending support capable of keeping the world turning while it stands on its own two feet, not even moving, but I think everyone will be tired done exhausted from hearing how you suffer through hours and lives because all you really do is repeat yourself constantly without ever saying anything else and even in this moment you're convinced, you always have been, that if they knew that today you are different, how you've just learned to suffer in a different way, they would understand that you can't handle any aggression that it shakes you to your core to remember that in this life everything is worth so little, that you are a woman who is not the woman they see before them and today—especially today—you are scared of being capable of hurting yourself by mere thought or of crying because some hand that reminds you of him might just touch your face or even of suffering for the sake of suffering alone, because today you are just plain scared.

MÒNICA BATET

"There Was a War"

(fiction)

Translated by Harriet Cook

The man sitting across from me asks, Did you know there was a war? I say that I do and we speak for a short while. Then I turn to look at those people who, like us, are spending the afternoon in one of the square's many cafés. And that's when I see him. He appears out of nowhere, walking as though he's got an enormous, invisible weight bearing down on his shoulders. He's dragging a rifle and when I look at his feet, I realize he's not wearing any shoes. He's a soldier and his face is covered in dust and blood. I can't stop staring as he limps along. I'm scared he might fall. He's moving closer and closer to our table and when he arrives, he stops. As soon as he opens his mouth, the square empties. Only the two of us remain, facing each other. He speaks in a language I don't know but am inexplicably able to understand. He tells me, A few minutes ago two of my mates died right in front of me. I'm sure I died afterwards too, but I can't remember. I've seen so many things, so many unimaginable things. Since all this started, I haven't been able to sleep for more than three hours at a time. The sound of bombs exploding keeps ringing in my head. You've got to be careful because they go off everywhere. I didn't want to go at first, but those men in the thirty-second ads on T.V. convinced me. When I told my wife, she cried. My mom cried, too. And they both assured me that, in the end, if I did decide to go, they wouldn't be there to see me off.

I left on my own one day at six in the morning. I made friends right away and for a few weeks it felt like one big adventure. Then we reached the woods and uncertainty filled the air. That's when the dying started. We'd wake up in the morning and look at each other, wondering who was next. Sometimes everything was covered in ash and the smell of death would cut through my breath. I couldn't put that smell into words even if I tried. When everything got to be too much, I thought about her, my wife who never wrote. I often closed my eyes just so I could see hers.

I wanted to escape so many times, but I always feared that if I did, I wouldn't be able to go home. I started to live my life feeding the only hope that gave me the strength to bear the cold and my mates disappearing one by one. I wanted to believe that it was a matter of time. We'd surrender soon or the others would, and I could go back to sitting in this square like you are now. It's bleak when what you hope for never materializes. For a few weeks now nobody has spoken. It's as though we're all scared of saying what we're thinking out loud. We're tired and there's a certain emptiness in our eyes. We're machines trudging through a night that never changes. We eat little, we try to sleep, and we shoot if we think the enemy's in front of us. Today could have been like that too, but there's a rumor going round that we've lost and the others won't be cruel.

We've just hurried down a deserted highway, entertained by possibilities we couldn't allow ourselves to think about yesterday. And that's when the shots started, far off at first and then closer and closer. I heard people crying out and watched as the blood from mutilated bodies stained the road red. When the two guys in front of me fell, I knew I would too. I'm twenty-five years old and I won't be able to see my wife again. I'll never have the chance to tell her that I shouldn't have listened to those ads. I won't have children and when I walk through this square, nobody will see me because you'll be off in another city with your friends. Then, he walks off, limping in the same way he did when I saw him arrive, and the square slowly starts to fill with people. My friends carry on talking without noticing my silence, and when one of them looks in my direction, I smile, trying to hide how I feel like crying over the death of a man I never knew.

"El mundo en mis manos" | Elisa Munsó

MARIA PILAR SENPAU JOVE

"The Bookseller"

(fiction)

Translated by Kate Good

He never felt like a lucky man. He didn't remember having ever scored a goal while playing soccer in the schoolyard as a boy, although, if he really thought about it, that might have been because they never passed him the ball much in the first place. Things were no better with girls. As a teen, he liked one in particular who sat in the back row and had bright red nails. A few minutes after math class started, her eyes would drift away from the board and, with a faint smile, she'd stare at something only she could see. He never knew if it was just the sky. One day, the girl stopped coming to school; they said she was sick. Maybe she was, because a few months later he saw her in the park pushing a stroller. She was pale and walked along looking at the pigeons. Years later, he got married. His wife was a good woman and always had the house ready in case anyone dropped by, even though he never dared to ask who she was waiting for. At night, when he couldn't sleep, he'd turn on the lamp on his nightstand and, while waiting for sleep to set in, he'd look at his wife's hands. But she never painted her nails. Then he'd try to fall asleep thinking of that girl from class.

His father died when he was a teenager and he'd had to start working. He found a job as a cashier at a neighborhood bookshop. Since he wore glasses and knew how to listen—well, more than listen, what he did was stay quiet while others were talking—people started to trust him and ask his advice about books. One day, the owner of the bookshop, who was getting old, offered to sell him the business. His wife encouraged him to take her up on it. Well, more than encourage him, what she did was humiliate him, as if she were suggesting that if he let this opportunity slip, he wouldn't have another. Maybe she was right and this would be his only chance to own a business, although what he really wanted was to run his own hardware store, a place where everything sold is exact: nails, screwdrivers, hammers, wire. Precise tools to fix specific things; one need only know the proper measurements. He adored that infinite world of tools and metal wires. Whenever he could, he'd spend a good, long while looking at the hardware store display just up the street from the bookshop. On days when he was sad, he'd walk in to buy something; afterward, on the way home, he'd press the little object against his palm and relish the feeling of security found in the thing so intimately connected to himself.

Once home, he'd pull out his toolbox, open it, and gaze trance-like at the screwdrivers assembled like scalpels, the nails of various lengths, the browned handles of the hammers. . . . He waited, motionless, until this scene settled inside him, and then he'd shut the box, satisfied—not from greed, but like a man conscious of the value of objects. If he could only own a tool store, then after dark he'd pull down the metal shutters and feel the true dignity of men, compressed into that one moment. But when the soul is empty, fear is far-echoing, and so he decided to take on the bookshop.

Despite all the years he'd worked there, he had never read a book; his only connection to them was taking them out of the box and displaying them in neat piles around the shop. When someone asked his opinion of some author, he always said they were good. What else could he say? He put his faith in the publishers' yardstick. Besides, who was he to criticize? Those who came in to buy something without knowing what they needed had bad enough luck as it was.

When someone approached to have him recommend a good book, he'd lean in a bit like he'd (often) seen the Marist brother do at school and assess the danger, and, like the Marist, he'd respond by asking a question; that would buy enough time to make him appear to be thinking. Then he'd pick a title at random from one of the tallest piles and, imitating the fishmonger's gesture of distinction, he'd show it to them. Moreover—and this he was indeed careful about—he tried to choose a pretty jacket in case the book had to spend time on a customer's bedside table. Only if the book were for a child would he really make an effort; he knew the impact a story could have. A story wasn't a toy; a story was an introduction to the whir of the world and it was important to choose the right tool. Only then, conscious of the danger, would he turn his back and walk up, gladiator-like, to the shelf of storybooks. When he was little, he got *Capitán Trueno* as a gift on Three Kings Day and, naturally, it had soured his existence. If only they had given him the one about the ugly duckling, perhaps his life would have turned out differently.

The days passed and everything went along more or less as always at the bookshop. It was toward the end of October, when the air was just beginning to chill, when, by mistake, they brought him the box of books. He opened it, and seeing poetry inside, he planned to return the box the very next day. It was a product that didn't sell well. But that title, *Strangely Happy*, surprised him. Without knowing why, he took them out and placed them in a pile next to the counter. That afternoon, while buzzing around the shop, he'd turn his back from time to time to look at the books of poetry, and, in a low voice, as if speaking privately with the poet, he'd tell them about his clients and his wife. Little by little, he grew accustomed to their company, despite having resolved that if he didn't sell any he'd return them the next month. On nights when he awoke in a startle, he'd think again about the poetry book, no longer needing to switch on the light to go find his mother like when he was little. Strangely, he'd fall back asleep as if someone were watching over him from somewhere inside the book. One day, a boy walked up to the stack of poetry books, took one, and proceeded to leaf through it; after a few minutes, the boy's eyes lit up and when he came up to the register, the bookseller spotted—somewhere, in the glint of his eye—the hardware store.

Months went by and he still hadn't returned the books. One day, a middle-aged woman picked up another one, and as she was paying for it, the bookseller noticed her red nails. After she left, he gazed at her through the shop window until she disappeared from view. Meanwhile, inside the bookshop, the angling afternoon sun began to cast long shadows over the wooden floor. He shot a knowing glance at the books of poetry and then, suddenly, all was calm. Solemnly calm.

The pile of books remained by his side, diminishing little by little, like water evaporating from a pond in winter. Until one day only one remained. Without thinking, he gave a quick glance around him and hid it under the cash register. When he felt lonely, he ran his hand under the register, touching the book with his fingertips, like one would feel for a revolver while walking through a neighborhood that's dangerous at night.

That afternoon, his wife left him. She told him she didn't love him and he didn't ask why. On his first Sunday alone, he went for a walk far away from his neighborhood. He spent a long while walking alongside strange houses, until he suddenly remembered the book of poetry. It was already late by the time he made it to the bookshop. In the dark, not wanting to turn on any lights, he put his hands under the cash register until he felt it. He waited a few moments, motionless, feeling the charge of what only the soul can see. He removed it slowly, put it in his coat pocket, and walked home. Once home, he pulled it out of his pocket with one swift gesture, and, book in hand, he searched the house looking for the perfect spot for it. There weren't any other books, and, all on its own, it would be too obvious a peephole for any busybodies that might drop in. Suddenly his toolbox came to mind, and with all the delight of one who has just found the perfect hiding place, he went to the living room cabinet, took out the tool box, and placed the book near the bottom, on top of the screwdrivers.

Now, every night after dinner, he sits down in the living room awhile, takes out the toolbox and puts it in his lap. With the earnest familiarity of an expert, he removes the book, opens it, and looks for a poem; not just any poem, but one in particular, because he knows every screw needs its bolt. He reads the poem, then closes his eyes and waits for her to appear; strangely, she doesn't sweep and her nails are painted passion red.

ALBA DEDEU

"Porcelain"

(fiction)

Translated by María Cristina Hall

It's late, today, when she asks me to leave the kiln on the minute she walks in.

"No worries, I wasn't turning it off."

I tell her I'll be needing it a few more hours today. Five-hundred mice to make: there you have it. And tons of unpaid overtime, of course. Why would I even bother asking? Manel and Joan Lluís got nothing for their extra twenty hours last month, when they had to finish up those damned pots for the fair—and it'll be no different for me and my porcelain baptismal mice.

The windows rattle like chattering teeth, and the sky, too bleak for this time of day, pitches a storm. Cecília doesn't look amused at my staying but says nothing. She rummages through her locker for a while, picking out molds from the shelves. She doesn't like people poking around in her locker or meddling in her work, and she's looked daggers at me more than once for getting too close.

Joan Lluís sweeps the floors and rants to his father about the last time Mrs. Gregori screwed him over. He still hasn't caught on to Cecília's presence—breaking off mid-sentence at the creak of her locker, right when he was about to compose a most genteel epithet for Mrs. Gregori. But Cecília just turns to him blankly:

"Well don't mind me. You can go ahead and say it."

Joan Lluís gives a sheepish titter and goes on sweeping quietly. Cecília scares him a little. When she first started coming to the workshop, we all assumed she was just a spoiled girl taking up ceramics on a whim. He would sweet-talk and ogle her—until one day she aimed a merciless stare at him and told him to leave her alone. Joan Lluís took her words to heart. Now that she's already learned everything there is to know and can get by on her own, he just looks at her from far away—just like his father does.

I decide I'll risk her scolding and carry my box of mice over to the table beside her. But she holds back: maybe she isn't peeved at my company today. I take heart and drop in on her table, where she's wiping the molds she picked out from her locker. There's one mold for each arm, one for each leg, and one for the head.

"What are the arms doing?" I probe, guarding my tone.

"They're drawing a bow and arrow."

"Heading out. We're done for the day," huffs a tired-looking Manel. He and Joan Lluís walk out the door quietly, letting a draft of cold air scamper around the shop.

With just the two of us left, only the clinking figurines I pull out of the box break the silence, until I have them all laid out in front of me. I guess the Pied Piper must have felt like this. Then I notice Cecília peering at me from the corner of her eye as I ready my paints, and she asks me when the order's due. Tomorrow morning? Tomorrow, yeah. We go on working and say nothing to each other for some time, listening to the bluster that whistles through the hinges on the top windows. A few minutes later, a light flashes through them, and when the thunder strikes, our eyes meet and she makes a face at me, playing scared. I'm so struck by the change in her usually deadpan expression that I burst into laughter. The thunder roars on and the occasional specter of lightning bounces off the walls, but the rain holds back. It hasn't even been fifteen minutes since the first thunderbolt when Mrs. Gregori barges in.

"What are you still doing here?" she barks at Cecília.

I'm stuck with my paintbrush in the air, petrified. Every time this woman walks into the workshop, our blood runs cold—her icy draft profaning our sanctuary.

"I'm working, mother."

"I see," she retorts sarcastically. "You sure don't bring a lot of dolls to the shop, for someone who works so hard." She turns toward me: "So you're here to work, huh?"

I decide to pretend I'm not the one being addressed and just lower my gaze—I'd rather not take the hit. Cecília goes on polishing the molds cool-headedly and doesn't look up either. When she's done, she lines them up on the newspapers, picks up a bottle of porcelain, and starts pouring its milky white liquid into a container.

"Are you listening to me?" Mrs. Gregori snaps.

"Yes."

"Then answer me!"

Cecília opens a small metal box, measures out half a teaspoon of iron oxide, and sifts the rusty powder into the container.

"I don't know what you want me to say," she replies as she stirs the liquid. "When I do bring more dolls, you say they take up too much space and don't sell."

"No. The real problem is you're a liar, or worse." Mrs. Gregori glares at her scornfully, making sure to pause long enough to let her implications settle in with their full weight. "Your aunt and uncle are coming over for dinner tonight, so I need you home by nine. And wear something nice, for God's sake. You've been disgusting lately."

"Okay," she replies, impassively, and goes on stirring the porcelain as its immaculate white gives way to a fleshier tone. Mrs. Gregori casts me one last venomous glare before she walks out the door without a goodbye.

Now that the porcelain's blended at the right tone—like rosy skin— Cecília carefully sieves it into the molds and runs them over the container, letting the excess porcelain drip back in.

"Why do you let her treat you that way?"

This is one of those times she could very well flash me one of her icy glares, kind of like her mother does, and tell me to mind my own business. But she doesn't even lift her gaze. It's as though she hasn't heard me, focusing all her attention on the porcelain dripping from her mold.

"I'd get with you just to make her mad," she says without facing me. "At least that way she'd be right for once."

This doesn't really sound like a proposal, but I indulge in the fantasy, if only for a minute. Mrs. Gregori says Cecília looks disgusting—and that isn't really the case. It's true that she's skinny and has none of the usual womanly curves, and she usually looks like she threw on the first thing she could find. Sometimes, her hair falls over her face and she just shoves it behind her ears without an inkling of flirtation. But still, her pale features, which hold no charm in particular, possess a certain strength, a steadfast focus that attracts me.

Lightning flashes across the sky once again, and a thunderclap makes the windows ring louder than before. Cecília rests her brimming molds on the newspaper and gets up to grab a sweater from her locker. Then she comes and hovers over me, watching me paint the mice's eyes and tails blue and gold, their mouths and whiskers, black. A little inscription goes on the animals' left flank: "Marc's Baptism 6/22/20—." Cecília sighs.

"She wants to stop paying you commissions for the porcelain figurines. And you won't even have to worry about it for too long—she's having me take over that as well."

Her words hit me like a bucket of cold water. With the economy in trouble, Gregori's been snipping at our salaries—and of course we can't complain—we just have to grin and bear it or lose the rest as well. Still, this thing about the commissions catches me by surprise. It makes my blood boil to think I'm being cheated of something that should be mine, and I don't know how to fight it.

"Great. Manel's going to throw a fit."

"Well he should be careful, because she's under the impression that she can replace you without a hitch."

I can't work with her rambling, and that impassive tone of hers gets me even more rattled—it's like she's just talking about the weather.

"You do know about Manel's wife, right? That they're about to lose their house because of her?"

"Yes"—now she looks me in the eye—"I do know. I told her I can't handle the figurines on my own. I have too much work with the dolls as it is, but when she gets something in her head there's no stopping her—there never is."

At that moment, the door bursts open yet again and Ecaterina walks in the room.

"*Buna!*" cries Cecília with a smile.

Ecaterina shuts the door and lets out a puff, her nose red from the outside chill. She ran here all the way from the store, she explains, out of breath. I can tell she's surprised I'm still here. I've usually been gone for hours by the time she arrives. Ecaterina sits down next to Cecília, opens her bag, and starts unfurling a jumble of needles, threads, and fabric scraps.

She's laughing but her eyes falter as she tells us she was late because Gregori bombarded her about how many dolls they'd made and how many hours they'd spent on each dress. Halfway through her story, though, she looks at me and hesitates. Then she starts speaking Romanian and averts her gaze so adamantly that I know it's me she's talking about. Cecília tries to stop herself from bursting into giggles—apparently exasperating Ecaterina, who now speaks in a whiny and somewhat irritated tone. In the end, Cecília shakes her head and laughs, muttering a few more words in Romanian. I don't think I'd ever seen her laugh before, or maybe I can't remember, but I'm surprised to see her this happy. She no longer strikes me as that standoffish girl who always works soundlessly in the corner. Then she picks up one of the molds and examines it top to bottom, showing it to Ecaterina.

"The archer's head," she says, this time in her Catalan.

"So you think Mrs. Gregori is really going to sell these Amazons of yours?" I smirk. "She's usually so classic. . . ."

"She won't sell this one. She won't even see it, in fact."

"Is it for your private collection?"

"Sort of."

"I didn't know you could speak Romanian."

"Ecaterina's a very good teacher."

Her teacher, however, refuses to acknowledge my presence: she threads her needle and starts hemming a little dress, pretending she isn't listening at all. Suddenly, a dry wind smacks the windowpanes and the rain starts lashing at the laminate roof with such force that soon enough we hear nothing other than its constant hammer. The hours come and go. Inside, as the rain keeps falling and the sky goes dark, the three of us hone in on our own painstaking tasks. Cecília and I take turns at the kiln. I go first and pull out a batch of one hundred mice, then she goes over and fires the pieces of her archer—already stripped of their molds—and I hear the click of the knob as she adjusts the temperature. She heads my way and sits down next to me. Without a word, she grabs a brush and starts painting the mice.

"There's no way you're finishing these by morning on your own."

Sometimes Ecaterina absentmindedly breaks into song and we just paint and listen, our heads bent over the figurines. The deluge goes on outside, and every now and then the too-close thunderclaps make us jump in our seats. Inside, though, I feel sheltered and connected. This is different from being with Manel and Joan Lluís, but I can't put my finger on exactly why. Today's company is perhaps warmer, more intimate. It's also true that my colleagues don't quite sing like Ecaterina, and they never offer to take a load off me—probably because they're also drowning in work. Every once in a while I take a peek at Cecília's hands: they cradle the mice so carefully you'd think she was holding a live creature, but I'm taken aback by her nimble brushwork. It's just baffling—I've been painting at least eight hours a day for ten years, and I still can't paint the way she does.

"Where'd you learn all this?"

She smiles and hums Ecaterina's song. I guess some people are just naturals who can pick up painting in a heartbeat—while it takes years of tireless practice for the rest of us. As luck would have it, Mrs. Gregori's daughter is the perfect craftswoman, and with everything staying in the family, Gregori doesn't even have to pay her for the work she's been taking from us! It's no wonder she wants us out. We should be glad she didn't have more daughters like Cecília. We'd be out the door by now.

We have the first hundred mice painted in just over an hour and they're ready to go back on the tray for a second firing.

"Give me a minute. My archer's probably ready."

She opens the kiln, pulls out the tray of doll parts, and sets it on her table as I stick my mice in the fire. Ecaterina comes close: the two of them fix their gaze on the doll's head—still white and hairless—and study it with utmost attention.

"Wait till you see her painted," whispers Cecília.

The mice, just like the doll, are porcelain and have to go through at least two firings: first at eight hundred degrees, and then, after a coat of paint, at two hundred. Our most valuable pieces, like the dolls, get a second coat—maybe even another one after that—and they have to be fired again after each layer. But my poor little mice are just party favors—you can tie a bag of candy to their necks and let them gather dust on some dank shelf, until they fall and break a few years from now or the next time you find a new apartment—which is why they only get the two non-negotiable firings, and presto, they're off to the store with a single layer of paint. No matter how simple, though, the great family of five hundred rodents for Marc's baptism—how this many people could possibly attend a miserable baptism, I don't know—will cost me hours and hours of sleep, today.

Some time later, the patter on the laminate roof scatters with the waning storm. Ecaterina gathers her things and announces that she's done for the day: her eyes hurt. I hear them whisper in Romanian. With a bag on her back but no coat, Ecaterina walks out into the dark, windy evening, and bereft of her song, the workshop goes dreary.

"It's ten till nine," I tell Cecília.

"I know, but I just want to finish the eyes."

When she finally gets up I've already painted another twenty mice, but rows and rows of these creatures still squint at me blindly, and I can't help but let out a sigh. Then she sits back down next to me.

"Listen, you really don't have to. You should leave—your mother's going to be furious."

"Oh, don't worry about it. I can be a little late."

But she isn't just a little late. Minutes fall upon minutes and I keep glancing at my watch so she'll notice, but she just goes on painting the black whiskers and gold and blue tails while I agonize at the mere thought of Mrs. Gregori's face as she sees Cecília walk through the door.

I'm not exactly sure when we started talking, but our chatter makes me forget about the time. This girl, whom I'd always found as cold and sullen as her mother, now speaks to me candidly and opens up about just how hard it is to live in the same house as that woman. And she tells

62

me about her sister, who is just like her mother, and about how she's dying to go live with Ecaterina in some small apartment downtown. But she can't do that yet, she says. Not until she's sold at least one of her high-end dolls.

"With Ecaterina?"

"Yeah. She lives in an awful boarding house and wants out as well. If she can get my mother to pay her for the dressmaking . . . between that, her storekeeping, and whatever I get from the dolls, we could make ends meet."

"So you're not selling them at the store?"

"No. I'm tired of working for my mother. I know a few collectors, and these kinds of things sell well online."

Then I ask her about the dolls, and she talks about them like they're her children. It takes her about a month's worth of free time to craft each one, and she has the porcelain and paint shipped from abroad. The hair is always real—hers, Ecaterina's, or another friend's—and she gets a professional embroiderer to detail the dresses, she tells me, proudly.

"They're one-of-a-kinds. I've put so much into every one of them, it'll be hard to see them go."

"The archer's a one-of-a-kinds as well?"

"Yes, but I'm not selling the archer. She's part of my . . . what did you call it? My private collection."

"And will I get to see any of these one-of-a-kinds?"

She replies with a laconic "I don't know" and looks at me like she's probing my character. Soon enough, the rain pours down once again, this time with no lightning or thunder. Two beeps announce that the firing is over, so I head toward the kiln and pull out a tray of mice. It's a little past ten. Her family dinner no longer has any bearing, and Cecília looks like she's in no hurry to leave. How long will she stay? And why the hell is she still here?

"All set!" She waves her paintbrush in the air like a triumphant flag. "Bring your next batch over, and there you go, another hundred mice in the kiln!"

Between the two of us, we arrange the painted mice on the tray and then she sticks them in the fire. We stand in front of the kiln for just a moment, basking in its warmth. Maybe she's staying because of me? I cast her a glimpse out of the corner of my eye and notice a smudge of gold paint on her cheek.

"Look, you got paint on your face," I say as I put my thumb on her cheek.

I think I feel her warm skin quiver, especially when, possessed by some brazen feeling, I not only don't lift my finger, but let another two graze over her skin, and then slide all three down her cheek in a hesitant caress. Cecília throws me a piercing glare, her eyes hardened in anger. I'm pretty sure she would have slapped me if she'd had the time. But she can't lift her hand and I can't pull back mine, because at that precise moment, Mrs. Gregori bursts into the workshop and sees us planted before the kiln in that ever-so-mistaken situation.

I pull my hand down in a flash, and Cecília turns to see who's there. Mrs. Gregori's shape in the doorway could chill anyone to the bone: she stands there drenched, with her usually coiffed hair plastered to her forehead and her fitted dress clinging to her lanky body—her brutal stare gone black from all the mascara running down her cheeks.

"You!" she explodes, her voice hoarse with rage. "You filthy whore! You're a rakish slut! A disgrace to this family!"

She closes in on Cecília as she speaks, and I shrink back, panicking before her kniving flood. Cecília doesn't budge. She only lowers her gaze and presses her lips together, as if she were struggling to keep herself from talking back.

"You never get enough, do you? Between him, that piggish whore, and Joan Lluís . . . You probably served it up for Manel, too!"

"Alícia, please calm down," is all I muster the courage to say as I try to steady my voice. That's how afraid we are of this woman. "I can assure you there's never been anything between me and Cecília: not today, not ever."

She runs her venomous gaze over me.

"Shut your mouth, you." She turns back to Cecília, who hasn't budged an inch. "You won't deny it, will you? So the rumors about you are true, then? You're that big a tramp?"

She finally lifts her head and looks her mother in the eye.

"It's my life and I'll do whatever I want. I don't think I'm a tramp for loving . . ."

And then everything happens at once. Without letting her finish, Mrs. Gregori lifts her hand and strikes Cecília with all her might. And Cecília, so frail, buckles over the nearest table—the one with the tray of freshly fired mice. She desperately reaches her hands out to clutch something to keep herself from falling, and that something is the tray. Then both Cecília and the tray crash to the ground, and the figurines, still warm from the kiln, shatter to pieces in a great quake of broken mice. I let out a bewildered cry, and Mrs. Gregori jumps back in shock, rubbing the hand she just flung at her own daughter. Then a wave of nausea sweeps over me as I notice the colossal diamond ring on that same hand.

"Cecília, here, Cecília! Get up. Are you okay?"

But she just lies there, huddled on the floor, speechless. She grips my arm as I help her up and sweep her hair back from her mouth. She pats the wound with her fingers and looks at them. There's a trembling cut on her lower lip, and a dark trail of blood oozes down her neck, making its way to her sweater. I can't get her to stand straight. She's pale and her legs give way. She must be dizzy from all the blood.

"Ecaterina will no longer be working at the store," Mrs. Gregori announces, tripping on porcelain as she pulls back, unfazed. "I don't want to see her in the workshop again. As for you, you'll work at home from now on, and whatever needs to be done here, the boys will take care of. Understood?"

Cecília doesn't say a word. She's still clutching my arm, using her other hand to prop herself up against the table as she fights the urge to look at her mother. A sob escapes her, but just one.

"Understood!?" cries the authoritarian Mrs. Gregori.

"Yes. . ." Cecília mutters in the end.

The windows rattle as Mrs. Gregori finally slams the door behind her, but the ensuing silence, that muted quiet of rain, weighs down on us like lead. Cecília lets go of me and drops to her knees. She stretches out her arms and starts gathering the mice scattered about her, making a little pile of shattered porcelain.

"What a disaster!" she says, faintly. "What a disaster!"

I bend down and pick up a mouse's head. Its mouth and whiskers are painted exquisitely: she must have done this one. Cecília heaps the shards together and the pile grows taller and taller as she rambles on about the disaster, and then blood starts dripping on it, too. I'm feeling queasy, and now that it's too late, I'm filled with regret for having touched Cecília and caused that look of hate, and I'm even more sorry I did nothing to stop her mother from hitting her. I'm at a loss as to how I can comfort her, and while she's down on her knees, I do nothing but stand there uselessly, staring at her with my heart still shrinking. And she keeps on crying and whimpering, not because she was hit, not because her friend was fired, and not because of her own predicament as an exploited house worker, but because of the broken baptism figurines!

"Listen, Cecília, come on. Leave the damned mice alone. There's a first aid kit in here somewhere. I can fix you up a little."

"What a disaster!" she cries again, disoriented.

"Damn it, Cecília!" I snap, and hastily make an effort to soften my tone. "Come on up, let's get you off the floor. . . ."

I pull her up with one arm, surprised at how easily I can lift her tiny, trembling body. She obligingly lets me steer her to the little cupboard and makes no objection when I sit her on a chair and dab her mouth with gauze. But it doesn't help at all. Her lip keeps oozing blood, and it goes on trickling down her neck with every passing moment.

"Hold this gauze up against your lip," I instruct, taking her hand and placing her fingers on the wound, "Like that, put some pressure on it for a minute."

I can't tell if she's listening. She stares blankly ahead, and even though she presses her hand firmly against the gauze, her body seems inert, as if the strength had been sucked out of her.

"I'm going to go clean this mess up, okay? Just stay calm and sit still."

With the thrust of the broom, the scraps of porcelain screech against the floor like the shrill cry of some small rodent. Drops of blood speckle the ground and table, and I clean it all up with the cloth we use to polish the figurines. I turn to look at Cecília every now and then. She seems to be calming down. She's still huddled up in her chair, pressing the gauze against her lips, but no longer looks like she's in a trance. As I'm throwing out the shards of porcelain, I try not to think about the hundred mice that have gone to waste, except I can't help but feel hopeless, because if I recall correctly, there's only one small box left in the store, meaning I only have fifty left. Oh, God! What'll I do when they come pick them up tomorrow morning? With any luck, if I finish doing all the rest, I'll still only have four hundred and fifty. And maybe Mrs. Gregori will refuse to remember she's the one who got us off schedule in the first place, and then she'll try to calm her furious clients by billing *me* for the broken mice. Or worse—I might have to do like Ecaterina and find myself another job.

"Esteve."

Her voice is so close it startles me, tearing me away from my qualms. Her lips, though very swollen, have stopped bleeding. She sets her eyes on the shards of porcelain I just threw out—half buried in the dust and workshop waste—and I worry she'll start raving on about the disasters again.

"Don't think twice about it, Cecília. I'll figure something out; there might still be a full box in the warehouse."

She shakes her head.

"There's only a crate of fifty. But I was thinking there's something else we could do."

"Oh, yeah?" And really, on a night as bewildering as this one, I wouldn't be the least bit surprised if she were to open her locker and tell me she always keeps a stockpile of two-hundred mice—all painted and fired—just in case.

She pulls her purse out of the closet and lays the archer's parts inside—each piece wrapped in a separate cloth.

"Yes. Could you come to the warehouse with me for a minute?"

One of the less practical things about our workshop is that the warehouse is in a completely separate building, a few blocks down. So whenever we fire a batch of cooking pots or vases or anything, if we're not ready to take them to the store, we have to haul the stock over to the warehouse with a pushcart, precariously rolling it around the narrow sidewalks. Mrs. Gregori says she can't afford a bigger location where we could have the warehouse and workshop in the same place, but she doesn't want anything cluttering up the workshop either. Everything has to be stored in the warehouse, clean and tidy. If a pot or plaster angel cracks on the way, then it must be that we're clumsy—and she'll take it from our check.

When we get to the warehouse and I wield my key into the lock, Cecília stops me.

"No, no. Come this way."

We circle the building and arrive at a side street. Cecília makes her way up a flight of stairs that goes straight to the second floor. There, she unlocks the door with a key she wears around her neck and flashes me a mysterious smile. We walk in, and right away, I can tell I've never been here before. We rarely go up to this floor: we only store a few sacks of plaster and cleaning supplies up here. But I'm positive I've never seen this room. Cecília switches on a light and I run my gaze across the small, tidy room brimming with cabinets and cupboards full of boxes.

"This is my private warehouse," she announces, and that guilty smile on her beaten lip troubles me a little.

She picks up one of the boxes and carefully sets it on the ground, and as she opens it, she unveils a whole slew of little boxes. She pulls them out gently and shows off their contents without masking her pride. There's a small porcelain turtle in every one of them, each meticulously crafted. With their marvelous shapes and peculiar color combinations, I'd even dare say they're exquisite, showing such dexterity that I must admit I feel a little jealous.

"*Turturică*," she pronounces, gazing at the one in her hand as if it could come to life with the sound of her voice. "I have exactly fifty. With the fifty mice downstairs, that makes one hundred. Isn't that lucky?"

We study the turtles for a while longer, and she shows them to me one at a time, pausing to tell me a little anecdote about each of them.

"Ecaterina loves turtles. I was going to give her these on her birthday, but it's still a while away. I can make new ones."

"But the molds, did you save them?"

She shakes her head.

"I wanted them to be one-of-a-kinds, like the dolls. . . ."

I shake my head obstinately and start stuffing the figurines back in their boxes.

"I won't hear of it, Cecília. We can't just sell these turtles by the pound like party favors and tie little candy bags to their necks. Please! I'd be mortified! No, no, I won't hear of it! Marc's parents asked for a box of mice, and they'll get their damned mice and nothing more."

"You're still missing fifty," she probes. "The turtles are just the right size, and there's enough space for the inscription on the shell."

"No, no, no. Manel must have some leftover chicks from last week, or maybe those cats. . . ."

Now she's the one shaking her head.

"Ecaterina sold them all this week."

"How could she sell them if they weren't painted?" I hesitate.

"They *were* painted." She lowers her gaze and I catch her cheeks burning red. "My mother had me paint them; she was in a hurry to get the orders done. . . ."

I can feel my blood boiling over and almost work myself into a huff, but when I look back at her swollen lip my anger fades as quickly as it came. Cecília shuts the box and signals me to pick it up. I still can't wrap my head around the fact that she's giving up these gorgeous turtles, that I'm letting her sacrifice her treasure to save me. Now that she seems to have forgotten everything that went on just a while ago, she looks serene—so serene, in fact, it's almost disconcerting. I insist just a bit more. I tell her to save the turtles for Ecaterina, that they were meant for her, but she keeps cutting me off with a smile before she finally puts her foot down:

"Look, it's settled: we're using the turtles. This will all be over soon enough, and then I can make as many as I want."

I wait for an explanation, but she seems to be done. Then she heads toward the door between the cupboards in the back and pivots toward me.

"So do you want to see the dolls or not?"

The light clicks on. We're in a tiny room, almost like a closet, but it's pleasantly warm and gives off a scent of wood. Display cases line the windowless walls, and a dark fabric veils the cabinets on the right, hiding whatever's inside. Cecília's one-of-a-kinds deck the shelves to the left, and as I edge closer, all those sets of eyes peer into mine. Some have darker skin; some are black; some are very pale. I'm surprised their faces lack the childlike features of most porcelain dolls: their adult complexions steer away from those perpetually ditzy expressions—instead, they're so alive and human, it's disturbing. One of them sobs—her face warped to the point that real tears seem inevitable. Another bares her teeth in a terrible and maleficent smile, and the way she conceals her arms behind her back makes me dread her cruel treachery. Another laughs and thrusts her fist into the air, celebrating some colossal triumph. Yet another screams—her palms gripping her temples as her entire face coils in pain. The last one kneels, and my heart shrinks at the prayer I read in her pious countenance.

"God," I whisper. "Of course they'll sell. They're magnificent, Cecília."

She flashes me a proud smile as she unwraps her archer, carefully ensconcing each part in a wooden box lined with hay.

"And I assume your private collection is back there," I say, pointing to the hidden display shelves on the right.

She nods.

"Can I see?"

"Go ahead."

I pinch the fabric by its corner and slowly peel it back. Without warning, Ecaterina's pale, plump face appears smack before me. I jerk back in surprise, and the fabric swishes over the display case once again. Cecília bursts into laughter.

"Don't be scared, silly — it isn't real."

I pull the fabric back again and fix my eyes on the doll: yes, this definitely is Ecaterina's placid, smiling face, with that same, slightly bent, Roman nose, thin lips, full cheeks, and those constellations of freckles under her eyes. She's wearing a flowy country dress and an intricately woven pair of leather sandals. Tucked under a flower crown, her curls fall over her shoulders; her hair, with that precise orange, must be Ecaterina's. The doll sits on a bench and peers down at her lap: she's cradling a little turtle in her hands.

After hesitating for a moment, I inch back a second piece of fabric and another doll appears before me. This one is standing, her dark head of frazzled hair bowed to the floor as she stares down at her bare feet. She wears a simple, striped dress, and between the tresses of hair that fall on her shoulders, she wears a face of utter sadness. This is the same Cecília who took a beating just a moment ago, the same one who caved in to her mother's abusive regime with a word and nothing more. But now that I have the flesh-and-bone Cecília before me, I discern a far more vital expression on her face.

"There's more over there."

I push aside the rest of the fabric covering the first cupboard and come upon another Ecaterina. Tall and magnificent, she wears a long, immaculately white dress, with layers of embroidered silk falling down to her feet. A delicate wedding veil sweeps over her face and this Ecaterina seems too thrilled to smile. She peers through the silk with dreamy eyes, clutching a bouquet of minuscule flowers in her pale hands.

This time I don't wait for Cecília to remind me there are more dolls. I pinch away a hint of fabric from the second cupboard, and what a terrible sight I find when I unearth Mrs. Gregori's twisted face. Swollen and scarlet, with her jaw dropped open in a shriek that's been captured at the epitome of its horror, she's a monstrous spectacle, and her crazed eyes glare at me the way they glared at Cecília right before she struck her. The doll leans forward like she's hunching over her victim and thrusts an admonishing hand into the air.

"Do you like it?" Cecília smiles spitefully.

"Scary as real life."

Convinced I'll find another screaming Gregori or turtle-promenading Ecaterina, I finish pulling the fabric all the way up. But I wasn't ready for what I saw. I jerk back in shock and drop the fabric once more, aghast. Cecília snickers at me and tells me to get a hold of myself. I pull the fabric up again. This *was* another Mrs. Gregori indeed, but this time she'd collapsed on a chair as her features writhed in pain and shock. Her black and white dress-suit is just like the one the real Mrs. Gregori often wears. Three arrows pierce the doll's body but draw no blood: one on her left breast, one in her stomach, and one on her right side. The doll struggles to wrench this last one out. Her right hand clutches the shaft, her stout porcelain arm contracting in exertion. Perhaps her other hand made a lunge for the arrow in her heart but didn't make it and now lies limply on her striped dress.

Hypnotized by the doll's agonized expression, I don't dare look at Cecília. She draws the fabric back over the cupboard and covers this heinous sight. She peers at me vaguely, pale. Minus the wounded lip, this is the same aloof Cecília as usual.

"You might as well go down and fetch the mice. I have to tidy a few things up in here."

I obey without a word. Then I trudge back up the stairs, dump the crate of mice on the box of turtles, and just stand there, stupefied. They keep flashing before me, over and over: the angelical, beaming bride; the moribund Mrs. Gregori's twisted face, disfigured in pain. I stare at the boxes blankly, and my stifled brain refuses to focus. Until a box—smaller and darker than the others—catches my eye. This one isn't cardboard, but wood. I cave in to my curiosity and edge it off the shelf. I try to muffle the noise as I slip the cover off. Cloth lines the inside of the box. A little cushion that's made to shape nestles a metal bow, polished and glistening with pulleys at its ends. Beside it, a case holds three long, aluminum arrows, about twelve inches each.

A noise in the other room startles me. A hinge must have squeaked as Cecília opened one of the cupboards. I hastily shut the box, stuff it back on the shelf, and retreat to the doll room. Cecília stands behind an open cupboard on the right. With the fabric covering her, I can only see her legs.

"Cecília."

"What?"

"Will you let me see the archer?"

"I was just putting her away."

She opens a box, and inside, cocooned in hay, the arms are ready to shoot; the fingers, strained in effort; the legs, slightly bent, will steady her aim. Still lacking hair and eyebrows, there's a look of intense concentration on her face, and her forehead creases in a hunt for precision. Only the eyes are painted: wide open, attentive, and indisputably determined.

"Satisfied?"

I nod and head back to the other room. I pick up the boxes of turtles and mice, go outside, and breathe in the street's cold air. I sense the blue mountains circling the dark valley in the distance, hiding in the night. An icy gust sends a shiver down my spine.

"It's quite cold for June, isn't it?" Cecília remarks, standing at the doorstep.

"It really is."

"I wonder if it snowed up there. . . . I guess we'll know tomorrow."

"Yeah."

She locks the door and takes one of the boxes from me, smiling.

"Shall we go paint some mice?"

We make our way back to the workshop in silence. The houses around us are locked up and dark, the earlier storm drizzling down their shingles. Up ahead, the workshop's top windows give off a vague, hazy light. I realize with dismay that my fingers have gone numb from the chill and excitement: painting with cold fingers can be a nightmare, and sometimes it's just impossible. But then I remember we left the kiln on—thank God—and that the workshop must be warm. As if she's just had the same thought, Cecília smiles, and then, ever so quietly, she starts humming Ecaterina's song.

LAIA MARTINEZ I LOPEZ

From *Venus Spins*

(poetry)

Translated by Scott Shanahan

riders	ills	fever	April
charmers	players	one	asters
thirst	barings	October	disaster
riders	ills	fever	April
charmers	players	one	asters
thirst	barings	October	disaster
riders	ills	fever	April
charmers	players	one	asters
thirst	barings	October	disaster

Purgatory 33

Open your breast to the coming truth
and reach out your hands,
and bare your heart,
and broaden your mind,
and blow up your brains,
and hone your nose, tongue and ears,
chip off your lids and show me your eyes.
Gut your soul: swell it!
An alien just touched down on your balcony,
ships and all.

I inherited the well-turned phrase,
but they shortened—my name,
and I grew up just a chatty child.
If, for all she said, she didn't escape
the whips, the hooks, or the stake,
if her god could only just cover up
her dignity with snow,
for me, a defiant youth, death
awaits, bloody and unkind.
The cyclogenesis has been foretold.
But I will step forward and declare
—freely: this Love,
I will not gag it, even
if my mouth, crow-filled,
doveless, should burst.

Silence: the earth will give birth to a tree.
        Altazor, Vicente Huidobro

My nightmares have so much flesh
that I wake up in a sweat, as though I'd let you inside
a rainy season in India, and I recall
just the smells—your voice, a sitar—
And me as mighty cow, offering me up to day.

These dead don't stink like dead.
The skinny moon bathes their faces,
and a bed of leaves brightens their sores,
and they smell of feathers from ravens and woodpeckers,

but, especially, rooting in the rocks,
in the rocks that make them at home in the holy grounds:
none of you will see a worm, or even a fly
the slime of no snail could wipe away their names.
And in August the roses bloom, too.

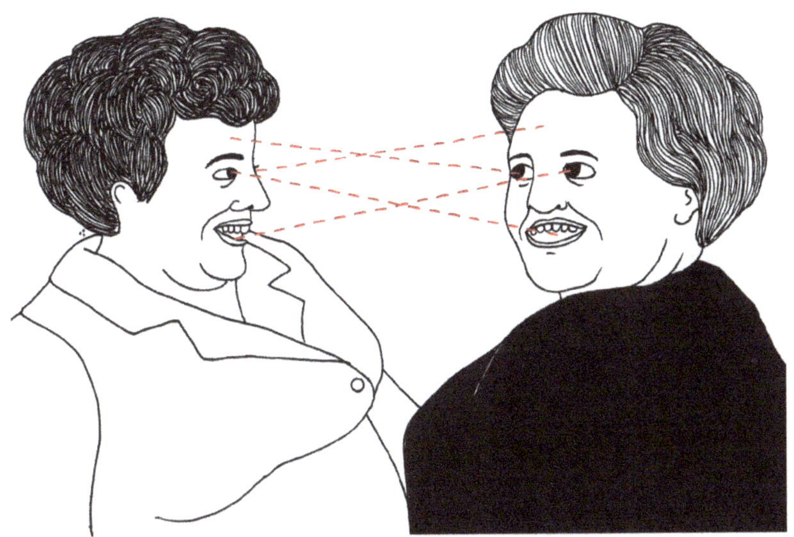

"Señoras Láser" | Elisa Munsó

M. MERCÈ CUARTIELLA

"Conxita and Mrs. Concepció"

(fiction)

Translated by Cortney Hamilton

One day, Senyora Concepció's husband asked her why they didn't have a housekeeper. The question took her by such surprise that, at first, she didn't know what to say.

"It's never come up," she finally responded. "Since I don't work and you don't like to spend money. . ."

Senyor Damià, her husband, was the type of man one could call stingy. He had an iron grip over the household budget: he made sure the lights were never left on; he hated to waste water; and he never turned the heat on before the first of November, nor the air conditioning until July rolled around, no matter the weather. He gave Senyora Concepció a bit to run the household, a weekly allowance with which she had to pinch every penny to cover the grocery shopping at the supermarket, placate the whims of her husband (who had a tendency to demand his favorite dishes once a week), and attend to the unexpected. If anything suddenly came up, if the dishwasher broke or the heating bill was surprisingly high, Senyor Damià would scrutinize the cost and the reason behind it. If he considered it just, he would dole out the exact amount, but not without first complaining that everything cost an arm and a leg and chalking it up to a miracle that they weren't destitute, with all they spent. In terms of what one could call spending money, to satisfy a small desire or a superfluous trifle, Senyora Concepció had none. Anything she wanted to buy required approval from her husband—a dress or new shoes, a necklace or some earrings—and was only authorized if he considered it necessary. For the small expenses—magazines or a small box of chocolates, an afternoon at the movies—Senyora Concepció managed relatively well, camouflaging them among other weekly expenses. But when the cost of what she wanted was too high, it was genuine torture to have to defend it before her husband, who attacked her with the argument that he did not spend the whole day at the office—working many hours and often getting home late—to have his salary spent on stupid, useless things.

With this system, Senyor Damià had managed to set aside a small fortune that his wife didn't know about; he had it in the bank, of course, in an account with a fixed interest rate. "A little nest egg for retirement," the man would say to himself when contemplating the bank statement. He also squirreled away a bit of cash in the house, in case of emergency, behind the cuckoo clock that hung in a corner of the living room. It was an antique that had been his grandfather's; old and worn out, the

clock had no value other than the sentimental. But Senyor Damià loved
it very much, mostly because it was his secret moneybox. Stuck in the
back, hidden from the eyes of his wife, in a brown envelope, were at
least 600 euros in fifty-note bills.

Fortunately for the couple, Senyor Damià was often torn between
his two obsessions: that of keeping up appearances among his cowork-
ers, neighbors, and friends, and that of his stinginess. This internal conflict at times forced him to authorize (with disgust) certain expenses he
would have otherwise considered completely superfluous. Like that of
the housekeeper. The issue had come up at an office lunch recently.
Senyor Cots, who stood above him on the corporate ladder, had asked if
his housekeeper had any openings, because his had retired and he needed a substitute. At first, Senyor Damià attributed this frivolity to the fact
that Senyor Cots was widowed and needed someone for the most basic
domestic tasks, which were unbefitting for a man of his standing; but
afterward, upon seeing that everyone was able to contribute a personal
anecdote on the matter (in spite of the fact that the hiring and supervision of these kinds of employees were done by the women of the house),
Senyor Damià felt duped.
All manner of progress had entered their home in this same way,
and Senyora Concepció was very grateful that her husband was so fussy
about what others would say and spent such great effort in giving the ap-
pearance that theirs was a comfortable and modern life just like anyone
else's. This resulted in things that in other cases one might consider basic, like central heating and air, a dishwasher, and some jewelry to wear
to the annual company dinner. Now, Senyor Damià had discovered that
he was the only one at the office without a housekeeper—aside from the
employees, because they shouldn't have one—and was ready to remedy
the situation.

"Tomorrow you will start to ask around and look for one, I don't want
people making a fool of me," he told his wife. "And one that doesn't
charge much, if possible."
Senyora Concepció cleared the table without a reply, and thought
to herself that the next day she would ask the neighbors; she seemed to
recall that Senyora Dolors had someone who came to do her ironing
and some of the more tedious tasks. She wasn't sure what to make of it
all. The only thing she knew clearly was that it did not give her any satis-

faction to think about having someone around her home all day, poking through her things, even if it was to clean them.

Senyora Concepció was initiated into the marvelous world of housekeeping the following afternoon, first in Senyora Dolors' doorway and then over a cup of coffee in her dining room, since Senyora Dolors' legs got tired from standing. For a good while, her neighbor convinced her that she would never find anyone as tidy and conscientious as herself—that is, if she herself was a good housekeeper. Senyora Concepció was quick to say that yes, she was very tidy and kept house well, and went on to explain a few of her personal tricks for removing limescale from the bathroom and for leaving the pots and pans gleaming.

"Oh, forget about all that, Concepció," the neighbor snapped. "What you will get, at the most, will be someone who pushes a mop through the bathroom and washes the dishes. Don't expect quality, that's all I have to say."

Faced with these assertions, Senyora Concepció began to worry. Senyor Damià was very particular about things around the house, to the point of being maniacal; she had gone through a terrible ordeal when they got married. Before she finally figured out how she should iron the creases of his pants and fold his towels, they had more than a few growing pains.

After Senyora Dolors' first long list of reasons why having a housekeeper was a universal cause for complaint, there came a second. It turned out that, not only did they not do the job well, but you also couldn't take your eye off them as they had a certain tendency toward laziness—and they charge a hefty sum, too!

"Between 10 and 12 euros an hour, sometimes," affirmed Senyora Dolors.

Senyora Concepció couldn't believe it. That much? She felt sure that Senyor Damià would never accept that kind of expenditure. She was also surprised that it was difficult to find a housekeeper, and that they weren't readily available, considering one could make so much doing what she had done for free.

That evening, Senyora Concepció presented the case to Senyor Damià. He wrung his hands as she assured him she had verified all the information, just as he had taught her to do with the price of anything before any expenditure. She was absolutely certain, everyone agreed on the costs.

"And how many hours does she have to come?" he asked, shaking like a leaf.

"It seems the norm is four to six hours," the woman responded, as she had also been informed of the customary frequency with which one contracted these services.

"We'll be ruined!" lamented Senyor Damià, saying that there was no chance of it happening, that he wouldn't be taken for a fool.

But in spite of this radical opposition, two days later, eaten up inside by the fact that he wasn't maintaining the same status as his colleagues, he gave in, bitterly telling his wife to look for someone.

"But educate yourself. She should be formal and hard-working. And watch her closely. Tell her that if we don't like her, we won't think twice about letting her go."

Senyor Damià wanted his wife to undertake this hiring as if she were selecting the lead actress in a musical; she shouldn't be satisfied with any old applicant, but should instead demand the best, keeping in mind the fact that they would have to pay her. For him, this expense, completely exorbitant and clearly not anticipated, was like a stab to the liver.

"All of this so as not to appear poor," he thought, and that evening, when he had finally made his decision, he went to sleep without drinking the glass of sherry he normally had after dinner, disgusted with the state of things and thinking about how he could recoup this new expense in his financial plan.

Senyora Concepció preferred to stay up mulling things over for a while and so sat in her armchair in front of the TV. It made her livid to think of paying a small fortune to another person to do the work she had done her entire life, at no charge and with excellent results. She found it absolutely unfair that someone would come and intrude in her domain and would take from her the position of housekeeper—it's not that she was crazy about mopping or dusting, but the house was her domain and she didn't want any intrusions—and on top of that someone who charged to do it! The longer she sat there, the more angry she became.

"If I'm doing all that, he should pay me instead," she concluded. That night she dreamt that she went to work at the home of Senyor Cots, dressed in a hairnet and an apron, and that the poor widower was so happy with the cleanliness of his bathrooms that he asked her to leave

Senyor Damià and come live with him, offering her an astronomical sum for her work.

Maybe it was the absurd dream she had that night or, in the end, the idea that was gestating unconsciously in her head; although it was a harebrained idea, it had its logic, and it would allow Senyora Concepció to solve more than a few problems. Sitting on the bed, once her husband had left to go to work—having gotten up, just like every morning, to make him coffee with milk and *magdalenes* (then remembering they were out and that she needed to buy more when she went to the bakery)—Senyora Concepció analyzed the issue at hand.

In the first place, her husband wanted, at all costs, to hire a housekeeper, regardless of the expense it incurred and the burden to their budget. In the second place, there was the question of her having done this job forever, and, on top of that, more satisfactorily. Because of this she found a certain indecency in paying good money to a stranger who, moreover, would snoop around in their private matters. For that kind of money, she herself could be someone's housekeeper, if her position allowed her.

And right then, the idea that was going around Senyora Concepció's head crystallized into a brilliant scheme. Naturally she couldn't be anyone else's housekeeper; she was a lady, and her husband, thank God, made a good living so she didn't have to work. But . . . could she do this job for herself? She had already been doing it for many years, only now she had the opportunity to charge for it. The thing was more simple than it seemed, so much so that Senyora Concepció was terrified some aspect of the question would escape her or get out of control.

All she had to do was tell her husband she had found someone, a trustworthy woman who charged, let's say, 11 euros an hour; not too much or too little, so as to not raise suspicions. He would spend the day out of the house and would never have to see her, meaning that she could maintain the farce without problems. She would keep cleaning as she had until now, and every week, she would earn 44 euros. It was perfect, and only involved a small and innocent lie that didn't hurt anyone. She was so happy that she decided to have breakfast at the cafe in front of the market that morning; instead of the fish she had planned on she would make meatballs for lunch and thus even out the expense, absorbing her little extravagance.

Senyor Damià wrinkled his nose and, at the same time, felt a weight come off his shoulders. The expense pained him, but in this way he considered himself fully in sync with his co-workers. If it ever came up again in conversation, at least he wouldn't look like a poor schmuck that has his wife on her knees, scrubbing the tile.

"Can I meet her, this woman? I would like to give her my approval," he said at the end of all Senyora Concepció's explanations.

"I will ask her, but I don't think so," she responded, nervously. She wasn't used to so much plotting, and she was afraid he'd pick up on her excuses. Improvising, she said she was very in demand and was only free from 11:00 to 1:00 PM on Tuesdays and Thursdays, which were the days she'd come. "If you could get away from work . . ." she added, taking a little risk.

Senyor Damià protested. The last thing he needed was to leave the office for this stupid thing.

"You are a big girl, it seems to me you can handle it yourself," he admonished her, as if she had requested his supervision.

And this is how Senyora Concepció's harebrained scheme was put into place, and the housekeeper came to be part of their lives.

Senyora Concepció learned to reallocate her tasks at home and leave the hardest for the days when Conxita came. She had given her this name as a private joke—Senyor Damià hadn't even noticed both women shared the same name, with a slight variation. Before, she would do part of the work every day: Monday, the ironing; Tuesday, the grocery shopping; Wednesday, the bathrooms, and so on, so as to not overload any one day and also because her well-ordered routine helped her work comfortably, without getting especially tired.

Now, however, everything had changed. Although she kept doing, as Senyora Concepció, some of the things she didn't do as Conxita— shopping, cooking, washing the dishes—she left the brunt of the work for the two days of the week when she assumed her alternate identity as housekeeper.

It should be said that she threw herself enthusiastically into the role, and that bit by bit, she added details to the profile of her new worker of domestic service. She, who had always dressed properly around the house, like the lady she was, bought a smock at the market and some plastic clogs. She, who did the cleaning with an apron over her good clothes, taking care not to stain them with bleach or splash any other product on herself, now undressed on Tuesdays and Thursdays and sheathed herself in a light and ample dress that gave her freedom of movement. She began to turn on the TV on the days when she was Conxita. The morning programs so criticized by Senyor Damià, classified as entertainment for the masses, were not appropriate for Senyora Concepció, but for Conxita, good heavens, of course she liked them. . . . She laughed and was scandalized by the shouts of the B-list celebrities, she cried and she anguished along with their televised dramas. Mid-morning she would take a break and, on more than one day, would lay down comfortably on the sofa with her feet up on the coffee table, allowing herself a little treat of chocolate cookies and sweet wine. She even lamented that Conxita didn't have her own cell phone to call in to enter the contests offering prizes as fabulous as they were absurd. She would be the queen with her own phone, she thought, and didn't rule it out for the future.

What's more, she was able to build up some savings. Before long it wasn't a problem to go out for breakfast or to the movies twice a week, even to the theatre one night when Senyor Damià was away on a business trip. She bought a new blouse that she had to swear she'd had for years, and was able to take her pearl necklace to have the clasp fixed, the breaking of which she hadn't dared confess so as not to endure a rosary of reprimands for her clumsiness, which incurred extra expenses. There was no doubt her life had improved noticeably since she'd hired a housekeeper.

Initially, Senyor Damià inspected the work of his new employee every Tuesday and Thursday afternoon, in search of something to criticize, but soon his obsession passed. He had to admit this witch who was costing a bundle did much better work than his wife. He didn't dare tell her so as not to offend her, but what a difference in the collars of his shirts, and how the faucets sparkled. He admired the clean windows and asked what kind of product she used, certain they had never been so transparent. He arrived at the conclusion that professionals had tricks that amateurs could never learn to master.

Disaster, however, arrived one afternoon, like the snake into paradise. The idyllic world of Conxita and Concepció lived in a precarious balance that shattered one ill-fated day when the housekeeper was sweeping the living room, and, it must be said, was distracted trying to guess which letters were missing in the panel on the TV screen, as the contestant hadn't gotten them right. Waving the broom around every which way, the top of the handle hit the one thing that Senyor Damià most loved, the cuckoo clock, which fell to the ground and broke. With the great crash, an envelope fell on the ground from who knows where. Conxita picked it up, contrite, and put it in the pocket of her smock without thinking any more about it. She was looking for the piece of the clock that had shot off to see if there was any way of fixing it, but she couldn't find it. Knowing herself to be fired, the housekeeper served herself one last glass of the wine Senyora Concepció kept for visitors. It wasn't until a few hours later, when she changed her clothes, that she remembered the envelope and looked to see what was inside.

That evening, Senyor Damià at first became red as a woodpecker upon seeing that the housekeeper had destroyed the cuckoo clock—that was the word that he used, "destroyed"—but then went pale as he felt the back of the clock.

"Explain to me exactly what happened," he demanded, white as a sheet. "You were here when that woman broke it, correct?"

Senyora Concepció confessed, visibly remorseful, that no, no she wasn't there, that she had taken advantage of having the woman in the house to step out for a moment to buy bread and, when she had returned, the clock was already broken. Conxita had shed a sea of tears after the accident and had apologized, begging for mercy.

"That we could even forgive a crime of this magnitude!" roared Senyor Damià, furious. "This woman must be fired immediately. And I want to do it myself."

"I'm terribly sorry, Damià, but I have already done it." And, in response to her husband's stupefied expression, she added, "I know how much you love your grandfather's clock and I couldn't stand for this type of carelessness."

That evening Senyor Damià didn't eat dinner, sickened by this turn of events.

Senyora Concepció tried to apologize, telling him that she had put too much trust in the woman and that she had been wrong, that she would keep it in mind for the next one they hired. Senyor Damià's eyes widened as big as oranges. "Another housekeeper? Have you lost your mind?"

Senyora Concepció, very serious for the first time the whole evening, argued that it was completely impossible, now that they'd tasted domestic service, to give it up all of a sudden.

"Plus, don't you remember why we hired her? Do you want to be known at the office as the poor schmuck who has to clean his own toilet? Or do you not care what people think of you?"

Senyor Damià stood up from the table. Never in his life had he suspected that having a housekeeper would cost him so much.

Senyora Concepció, on the other hand, smiled as she washed the dishes. She thought that the next housekeeper would surely be called Immaculada, and could charge 15 euros an hour. At the end of the day, Conxita charged such a good price because she was an amateur, but Immaculada wouldn't be.

TINA VALLÈS

"Taxi"

(fiction)

Translated by Jennifer Arnold

In the taxi, I'm overwhelmed by an uncontrollable desire to fly. I watch the city pass by in scenes and I'm overcome by such intense longing that I want to open the window, climb out, and fly above it, memorizing its every detail: the lady carrying her purse in a bag from Bonpreu, the child playing with a plane-tree leaf, the man talking on his phone and buying a newspaper without saying a word to the seller, the girl playing in front of a toyshop window, the old lady pushing a half-empty shopping cart that she uses as a walker, the old man passing time on a shady bench—all of them. In no time at all I'll miss these people of the city. It's not that I'm leaving, the taxi is just taking me to somewhere else, but never again will I see the city as I do now. The next time I look at it will be through different eyes, I don't know how, but that's how I imagine it: thus this desire to fly over the city. But I don't have wings, I have arms and hands that are, at this moment, holding onto my belly, which is so heavy that I'm afraid it'll drop and crack like an egg.

I'll have only been away for a few days but when I come back to the city there'll be nothing left of who I am now, even if I look the same on the outside—I'll be somebody else and it's no cliché. And I won't have become one of those magazine mommies with long straight blond hair halfway down their backs, who dress in white and smile even when they're asleep. I'll be an awkward monster with scars and an inflated chest. I'll look awful, wearing the first thing I can find that fits. I won't remember to brush my hair and I'll have left my smile behind in the operating room in the maternity unit.

That's right, I'm in labor—the moment all mothers eagerly await has finally come. All mothers. Yes, in a few hours I'll have given birth, or the baby will have been born, but will I be a mother? Me, a mother. . . . But that's not why I want to fly. It isn't to memorize the city I'm leaving but not. I want to run away. I can't be a mother. Maybe I should try moving my arms as if they were wings, and if my belly opens and the baby comes out, well, let it come out, because, right now, I don't know if I want it. No, that's not true, I do know; I don't want it. How can I have wanted a baby? How did I get myself into this? Right now it's a mystery. And I remember it was my decision.

And the scenes keep passing by and the city takes on those European colors as you cross Diagonal, and suddenly I start seeing those happy mothers from the magazines, but these women look real. Maybe they're wearing pastel colors instead of white, maybe their hair isn't naturally blonde and their smiles aren't quite so permanent, and there are moments when it seems to waver just a little, or even fade. But you can see from far away that they're happy mothers, and it's now very clear that I'm never going to be like them.

That's enough, that's enough I say. I open the window and let my belly hang. It doesn't hurt anymore. I feel my hands getting bigger, my arms getting stronger, my legs shrinking, my eyesight sharpening, my body getting lighter. I stand up, look out, and start to pull myself out of the car. I close my eyes, inhale the wind, consume it, and stretch out my arms with my feet on the seat until all that's left in the taxi is my luggage and my legs. My husband will be calling me to see what stage I'm at. We were talking about stages. . . . Because now my feet are no longer sinking into the seat. Now the yellow and black car is getting smaller, smaller, smaller beneath me and I hardly need to move my arms to fly. It's like lying dead in a pool, and I bite the wind and swallow it, devour it, and finally the city is below me, the city as I see it now, as I always want to it to be.

My belly's no longer heavy, though it hasn't changed. I can feel the baby moving inside, and, while I'm not really intuitive about this kind of thing, I'd say it's happy. But it's a happiness that won't last, because this is just a parenthesis and very soon they'll have me on the operating table and they'll take the baby out of my belly. They'll tell me it's my child and expect me to turn into a mother as if by magic and I won't know what to do. Then the moment will come when it'll open its tiny mouth and I'll have to offer my nipple and it'll suck. And I'll have to smile because it means that everything is as it should be, and that's what it's all about, being as it should. Performing, feigning happiness in front of visitors, crying when they go, because I won't be happy, not really. Everything will have changed, and everything will have shifted and they'll have taken everything from me.

But now I am flying and eating wind. I open my mouth and swallow the polluted air of the city that I'm about to lose and maybe it's not good for the baby, but then giving birth won't be good for me, and at this moment I can't think of anyone but myself. I won't have the automatic altruism that other mothers have, I, who, when I see a baby, runs a mile before they can ask if I'd like to hold it, because no, I don't want to hold it and if I admit that, then they all look at me as if I'd just confessed to a crime.

I never lose sight of the taxi that's taking my suitcase to the maternity hospital. In my bag my cell phone will be ringing. My husband will be beside himself wondering if I'm at the hospital yet, if he'll get there in time. He wants it, the baby, or that's what I've thought for the last 40 weeks that seemed an eternity and now I wish they were. Maybe he was also playing a part and now I'll find him flying like a bird up here with me.

Everybody gets pregnant; the mother and the mother-in-law talking about biological clocks and the spare room nobody knows what to do with. Suddenly all the pieces fit together and the picture on the puzzle is a child and that's the answer, because, well, why not? And flying doesn't bother my belly. I can hardly feel it, nor does it feel heavy, but the baby is still there and it's moving and I imagine it in the same position as I am, lying inside me. I say inside me but I'm not excited. What do you want me to say? To me it's just something that's moving in my belly, I have no ties to it and I don't know if I'll know what to do. I haven't sung songs to it, or talked to it, I've tried but it seemed so fake and I felt so ridiculous that I stopped right away.

I wonder if I could have the baby while I'm flying, give birth up here. If it's lying inside me then it could lie outside, and maybe if our relationship began with us flying over the city, it would change in just that moment. Everything would be better and I'd know how to play the role of a believable mother. I touch my belly, dig my fingers in, and push the baby's head downwards, shaking its legs hard, but nothing happens. So I fly and eat the wind and if it's polluted then so much the better, because I don't like the over populated European-ness of the city, with that mix of indiscernible smells and odors of waste, urine and rancid sweat.

Maybe if I turn over and, with sharp movements, fly closer to the buildings and the risk makes my adrenaline rush. What if I fly into a pylon, what if some . . . I realize I'm changing, until just a minute ago I'd never have dared put my life in danger for anyone, let alone for a baby I've never set eyes on, because what people say about looking at it and thinking it's the most beautiful baby you've ever seen, can't possibly happen to me. If this baby inside me is ugly, I'll know from the second I see it and no rush of hormones will blind me. And to me it'll always be ugly.

But the truth is I've started to change, as has the city. Now I see it as a world of potential danger and so I'm taken by the idea of giving birth in the air. I don't see it like I did a while ago. I won't look at it again as I

did before. And all because of this belly, because of doing what's expected of me, going along with everything, faking an excitement that doesn't
exist—if it did, it wouldn't make me happy. So I do somersaults, stop
listening to my body, and listen to my head. It tells me to pull myself together, get closer to the high roofs, absorb the waves from the antennas,
immerse myself in the smoke from the chimneys and extractors.

I swallow everything the city throws up into the sky because it's not
wanted, because I do want it and in exchange, I throw into the sky everything I don't need. It's a fair swap. My flying starts to make so much
sense that I feel movements in my stomach and I know the time has
come, that I'll give birth up here, among the clouds of pollution and
pigeons. I don't understand how, from so far up, I can hear a cell phone,
but I do. And I answer it. I don't know how I answer if I'm flying and
my phone is in my bag, in the taxi, and the taxi is down there, sliding
through the city to the hospital. But I answer and it's my husband wanting to know where and how I am. I say I'm in the air, that I'm fine, and
he doesn't know how to take it and asks to speak to someone else. And
I realize I'm in the taxi with my legs and trousers soaking, and the taxi
driver is looking at his seats, biting his tongue so as not to swear as he
steps on the gas, telling me to breathe, just like I've been doing, that it
seems like I'm gulping air and to keep counting, that we're nearly there.
And as I lose sight of the city, I can still see one of those happy mothers
walking along. I don't say goodbye, because when I see it again I'll be
pushing a stroller through its streets and I won't see it in the same way
I have up till now, as if I wanted to drink it all in. Instead, I'll analyze
it piece by piece, performing an autopsy with latex gloves and a mask,
dressed in white or pastel colors as I push a lock of dyed blond hair from
my face with a grimace that began as a smile.

Sólo ellas | Elisa Munsó

MIREIA VIDAL-CONTE

From *Ouse*

(poetry)

Translated by María Cristina Hall

OUSE II

not one day nor ten
would sate the Ouse
                    but twenty-one days

counting stones
Virginia of the waters
scars of our dread.

II

mother ushers
the water
seventy years of fright
beauty, yes!
the drowning cry
of a nonliably bodied
blackberry bush.

IV

The quiet of all that was written
without language.
ROSA FONT

you shell almonds
skin stunned fish
bursting
mouthfuls of cherry
a language sheared like
thistle bloom
dignifying
other rivers.

[UNTITLED]

you're two by the book's end
abandoned at intermission
unable to wolf it down
short of means and faith   as was she
you walk away with this failed
Ouse in your pocket.

[UNTITLED]

ANNA MARIA VILLALONGA

"Twists of Fate"

(fiction)

Translated by Natasha Tanna

She leaves her car in the car park and goes through the main door. She walks quickly towards the lift without stopping at the reception. They've already given her the details over the phone. Sixth floor, room 638. Unfortunately, she knows the place well. Her mother spends long stretches of time here and her stays have been almost unbearably frequent over the past few months. The elevator, which is crammed full, gorges on and spews out visitors on every floor, in slow-motion, while Marta simmers and seethes. Finally, with an unpleasant screech and a slight jerk, number six lights up on the display. Marta gets out of the elevator, walks past the empty security desk, and turns right. Room 638 is in an L-shaped area at the end of the corridor.

"Mom?"

A nurse is checking her fluids.

"We've sedated her," she says, with a neutral tone. "It's better to let her rest now."

"Oh, I see. Okay."

"The doctor will come by later and explain everything to you. If you need anything, press the call button."

Marta doesn't respond. The doctor. She can guess what he will say word for word. "You know the score—there is no treatment. Your mother has Alzheimer's and advanced osteoporosis. She gets confused, falls and breaks a bone. That's how it'll be from here on out . . . maybe you should think about getting her a wheelchair." Marta realizes that the situation no longer rouses any emotion in her. She's heard it too many times. She knows it's sad, but she can't help it. She sits down next to the bed and looks at her sick mother's face. She has unkempt hair, a pointy nose, and gaunt cheeks. A wheelchair? Maybe. What else could she do?

Suddenly, she hears a sob from the other side of the curtain that splits the small room in two. She gets up and turns around. The curtain's thin fabric is immaculately white, spotless. Carefully, she pulls it open at one end and peers inside. She sees a large, uncovered window and her mother's roommate, an elderly woman, in bed. Marta means to ask her what's wrong, if she needs anything, if she wants her to call the nurse, but the words won't leave her mouth. Her shock chokes them and they wither, suffocated in her throat as she stands there wide-eyed, her hands shaking.

But . . . but . . . what? No way, it can't be.

She feels her parched tongue and a bitter aftertaste belching from her stomach. Her head spins and her legs almost give way. She can barely breathe. Feeling faint, she grabs the curtain with both hands to stay on her feet.

The woman has drooping eyelids and a tense grimace. She's hooked up to a machine that measures her vital signs and the drip attached to her left arm releases liquid in steady intervals. She seems anxious. She writhes around whimpering, letting out little cries of pain. Marta takes a deep breath and stares at her uneasily for a long while. Then, when she feels she has somewhat regained her composure, she moves slowly towards the woman and looks at her from up close, arching over her. There is no doubt—it's her. The angular face, the ape-like expression, the muzzle that protrudes displaying a look of permanent irritation. And that vulgar, graying skin. Marta knows that those eyelids hide her light, short-sighted, slightly crossed eyes. She can't see them now because they are not fully open. Fuentes. That bitch Fuentes. The Gorilla.

What's happening? I don't understand it! But it can't be, it can't be.

The woman opens her eyes. For a few moments, it seems like she is looking at Marta, but she suddenly turns her head with a wince of pain. Marta knows her well enough to recognize those inexpressive blue eyes.

She has that look, and here she is. I can't believe it. I thought that . . . it can't be!

Marta runs her hand over her face, as if this might rid her of the torrent of feelings taking hold of her. A thousand images flash through her mind. Just like they did a month ago.

A year ago. Her whole life.

The nurse comes in to replace Fuentes's drip bag, which is about to run out.

"She needs a tranquilizer," she says.

Marta builds up her courage and nods at the nurse. She wants to see what she can get out of her.

"What happened to her?"

"She was run over in an alley behind the building. She's been in intensive care for a month, it's very serious—she has major trauma and internal bleeding. They just brought her to the ward yesterday, but she's still got a long recovery ahead."

The nurse stops talking and smoothes out the top of the bed sheet. Then she leaves. Marta is left alone. Major trauma and internal bleeding, but she's still alive. It sounds impossible. Marta casts another glance at the woman lying in bed and, like a wave, those treacherous memories overwhelm her, triggering that same old feeling, familiar, unchanged. A whole life carrying the burden of those insecurities, doubts, fears. A whole life of anxiety, romantic failures, loneliness. Despite the passing of time, which they say heals everything. Despite extensive therapy.

How can this be? Finding her here, at the hospital, in the same room as my mother.

A shiver runs down Marta's spine. She is soaked in sweat. The same old feelings that have destroyed her life remain intact, determined to survive. Just like Fuentes, who's still breathing.

Marta walks up to the window and stares through the glass, but she doesn't look at the moving cars or the reddish clouds of late spring. She sees only a cluster of boney legs clothed in a horrible uniform. She has just turned ten and, for the first time, finds herself at the entrance to the school run by nuns where Fuentes teaches. Marta doesn't know why but she feels intimidated as soon as she sees Fuentes, with her short-sighted eyes that look Marta up and down, her monkey-like face and those thin deformed lips, protruding like the hallmark of a bitter, intolerant person.

She soon discovers that the other girls call her "The Gorilla" and thinks the nickname suits her perfectly. She's shabby and ape-like; she looks like a primate dressed up as a woman. She's fully aware that everyone's scared of her. She is never nice, never lets a mistake go unnoticed. She demands faultless behaviour, adherence to needlessly strict rules upheld under all circumstances.

Marta closes her eyes. For years her memories have been hazy, blurry, diffuse, incapable of piecing together a coherent, continuous narrative. To stop her hands from shaking, she clings to the window sill. She knows that any minute now, uncontrollable images will emerge from the misty depths of her mind. Vivid. Unchanging. Like shreds of shame, of incomprehension. The silent and searing remnants of fear. Because of that woman, who now looks like a harmless creature in a hospital bed, her mind holds no comforting thoughts. There are just shreds. Shreds that dig deep.

She sees herself shake as Fuentes asks her a question. Despite having studied hard, she stutters fearfully and is unable to string two sentences together. She sees herself freeze up at the door to the lunch room, with her heart in her mouth, when Fuentes does not let her in because she has arrived five minutes late. She sees herself freeze up with panic on the side of the swimming pool while Fuentes, who is supervising, studies her from the other side of the pool with her worst grimace, a face full of scorn. And she, an insignificant insect drowning in her red swimsuit, splutters that she is scared of water, she does not want to jump in, she doesn't like swimming lessons. And she remembers those harsh words pronounced like a judgement. "You're a good-for-nothing. Useless. You'll never make anything of your life."

Marta tries to tell her parents about it but she doesn't know how. Those were different times. The teacher's authority went unquestioned. And in front of her parents, Fuentes was polite and proper.

I was just a frightened little girl, with nowhere to turn. Everything seemed so complicated, so difficult.

Her worst memory emerges from the mist like a mountain peak. The Monday that Marta arrived late to class because her dad's car broke down. She was twelve. She's sure of it. And it's winter, because it's cold. Fuentes doesn't let her explain, doesn't let her say a single word. She looks up from the book she's holding and pierces her with those light, short-sighted, slightly crossed eyes. Those icy eyes of an ugly monkey. "Do you see this girl?" she says slowly, exaggeratedly stressing every syllable and shifting her gaze to the rest of the class. "Do you see her? Well, she's a useless good-for-nothing who will never achieve anything in life. If she's not capable of arriving on time, what else can you expect? Nothing! She won't even be useful for wiping old people's asses." Marta, still standing in front of the class like a broken puppet, isn't able to hold back the single tear that slowly trickles down her cheek. Then, without realizing what's happening, she feels a strange heat between her legs.

She was so, so scared. . . .

Fuentes did not let her change. "See that? See how right I am? On top of being useless, she's also dirty. You know what, Dirty? Do you know what will happen to you? You'll never find a man who loves you. What man could love a dirty girl who wets herself?"

She makes her sit down and put up with the wetness for the whole morning. Marta's face is burning with embarrassment, but her legs feel icy, wet, sticky. Her own stench reaches her from under the desk, an acrid smell that becomes more unbearable by the minute. She gags. She's scared of throwing up then and there. The other girls don't dare look at her. They keep their heads down and focus only on their writing, as if they're trying to make time go faster. When the bell rings, Marta disappears in a flash. A wet, yellowish mark is left on the chair.

Fuentes grumbles and writhes between the sheets. She mumbles something, but it's impossible to understand what she's saying. Marta isn't listening to her. Just one thought resounds in her brain. Incomprehension. The question that's haunted her since she was young. "Don't look for a motive," the psychologist had insisted, "Psychopaths don't need motives for their behavior. They enjoy hurting others, full stop. Anyway, was she the same with the other girls or was it just with you?"

That didn't matter to Marta. Yes, she had seen Fuentes insult other girls but she always felt Fuentes was worse with her. Much crueler. Maybe it was Marta's mysterious instinct, possessed only by animals and children, that let her immediately understand Fuentes's true nature. When Fuentes looked at her with those piercing, expressionless, blue-green eyes, Marta trembled as if she'd seen the devil. Fuentes never did fool her. Never.

You could hide it when you wanted to, but I always knew you were crazy. You were dangerous. A dangerous crazy woman who destroyed me.

Marta tries hard to return to the present. She moves away from the window, short of breath. The spotless, white curtain splits the room into two small symmetrical sections. She doesn't know why, but that calms her down. She moves closer to the bed and studies Fuentes up close once again. She looks at her eyelids, wrinkled up over those myopic eyes. Her pale, parched cheeks. Her bloodless, lifeless lips. Marta feels disgusted, but gripped by a strange fascination. She can't stop looking at her, scrutinizing her. Rage bubbles up inside her, filling her mouth. Every beat of her heart rises into a rush of hate. Congealed hate. Hate she wants to spit out for good.

Fuentes is wearing a hospital gown, faded from so many washes. Marta parts the cloth a little and pokes a finger through to Fuentes's neck. It's yellowing. It's the flesh of an old woman, she thinks, a hideous old woman. She presses her finger firmly on Fuentes's face and it leaves a lighter mark that stays for a while before disappearing slowly, dissipated in the yellowish blue of her skin. Suddenly, as if Marta's finger has activated some hidden mechanism, Fuentes opens her eyes. Her light, short-sighted, crossed eyes. Marta steps back. Her body is tense, her vision blurred.

You fucking bitch, what are you still doing here?

Marta steps back from the bed, holding Fuentes's gaze. She asks herself how many times fate can work in her favor, unexpectedly. Very few times, she thinks. Then she chuckles to herself, because she understands that fate is, by nature, unexpected.

She takes a quick look around but doesn't find what she's looking for. The door to the bathroom is at the foot of her mother's bed. She goes in. It's tiny, but everything is aseptically clean. She sees two urinals hung on the tiled wall and two very neatly folded white towels near the sink. There is a bottle of soap and some surgical gloves on top of a small shelf. Marta smiles and looks down at her hands. They're no longer shaking.

Calmly, she pulls down her pants, sits on the toilet and takes a long piss. She pisses with an immense pleasure that causes her to let out a deep moan from the bottom of her throat. She closes her eyes and sighs. She unhurriedly enjoys the jet of warm liquid that powerfully hits the snow-white porcelain of the toilet. Then she gets up, pulls up her pants, and, with the same sense of calm, puts on the gloves.

She leaves the bathroom and hurries over to the bed. She feels incredibly tall. She's transformed into a giant who dominates the world from way up high. She slowly and steadily presses her right hand against that ape-like face. Her new giant hand squashes those eyes, that nose, that rough muzzle. Unsatisfied, she opens up her whole palm. Fuentes lets out a guttural sound, like a monkey's snort, while Marta separates her fingers so they let through the wild terror of that cross-eyed glare. Fuentes shakes in agony, she struggles, but she does not have the strength to defend herself. The gloves slip and Marta separates her fingers a little more. Fuentes's eyes have gone black. They are two holes that devour her, bewildered, terrified, uncomprehending.

Marta can't tell if Fuentes has recognized her, but she doesn't care. Just as she didn't care on that evening a month ago as her white knuckles gripped the steering wheel in the lonely alley.

"For You!" | Elisa Munsó

LLUCIA RAMIS

From *All That Died Among the Bicycles That Afternoon*

(fiction)

Translated by Megan Berkobien

Every Thursday, my father has lunch with l'abuela at her house in Palma.

We bought a roast chicken and l'abuela explained that, a long time ago, chickens were fed on fishmeal, that's why they'd taste like fish, and why the eggs would taste fishy, too. And years before that they'd deliver live chickens straight from the farm, from Felanitx.

Once, one of l'abuela's kids told her there was another animal in the basket, but she didn't pay it any mind. She left the large basket on the porch for two days until the stench became unbearable. Only then did she go take a look, and, sure enough, there alongside the chickens was a dead rabbit swarmed by flies. They'd deliver them dead like that because, if not, they'd piss all over. The household hated rabbit from that day on.

"Not just that, you also had to boil the meat to make sure it was still good. Back then you boiled everything just in case," my father said.

"In those days, entonses, they said it wasn't good to eat the chicken skin, it'd give you some kind of sickness, a terrible stomachache or something like that," l'abuela explained.

And my father added: "They'd say you'd turn into a maricón."

*

L'abuela had heard tell that when her father—a strong man with long legs—was a cadet, he carried Franco's backpack for him because Franco was too scrawny to haul it himself. Born in Ferrol, on the Galician coast, Franco had wanted to enter the Marines but they wouldn't admit him. According to his official biographies, the Generalísimo was first in his class, but that's not the truth. In my great-grandfather's Infantry Academy yearbook—he was an officer in the same year—Franco was ranked in the hundred-somethings. Even my great-grandfather was ahead of him.

*

My father and l'abuela argued a while over politics.

"Your friends," my father says.

She says: "They aren't my friends. When I was younger I thought politicians were missionaries fighting for the good of society—that they wanted to help us."

"That's their strategy," my father said, "to soft-soap the Army and Church so that people like you vote for them and think they're doing good. They've gotten to you. They're worse than Franco."

"And now what's Franco got to do with it?"

I whisper: "Papà . . ."

"They're bringing back the dictatorship, the oppression, like during the war. They're a bunch of fascists!"

"Papà . . . if you say fascists you'll discredit your argument . . ."

"What?!"

"Fascism is something else."

"Germans, Italians, Spaniards, they were all fascists. And they killed anyone who didn't think like them."

"Do you know what they did to the nuns during the war?" l'abuela asks.

"And do you know what they did to anyone who had ideas of their own? Do you know what they did to the leftists?"

"But there were people that first went one way and then the other without ever really thinking anything about it. Plus, your father was with the Nationalists," I say. "Are you saying he was a fascist?"

"Mumpare didn't kill anyone."

"You can't reduce an entire civil war down to a clash between the good guys and the bad. There were good and bad people on both sides."

"My father was twenty and my mother thirteen during the war, they didn't decide a thing. But there were people to blame, people who launched a coup because they couldn't bear that the democratic left had won. And those same sons-of-bitches are returning to power now because mother dearest voted for them."

When he speaks about the left, he does it in first-person plural; when referring to the right, he does so in second-person plural, implicating both l'abuela and me.

"Left and right are antiquated concepts," I attempt to argue.

"And capitalists like you, sweetheart, can't see the difference between the left and right, that's where we are at this point. That's the problem, we live in a society of savage consumption."

"Because Franco was a huge capitalist, right?"

"He's the only fascist that the Americans protected, and not for nothing."

"And better a Stalin than a Bush?"

"Better a Lenin!"

"Papà, being against one thing doesn't mean you're in favor of another! Even the socialists have blood on their hands."

"And what's worse? A fascist newspaper accusing socialists of murder without any proof or that Prime Minister Aznar killed thousands of innocent people in the Iraq War? How many people are dying of hunger under our current president? At the moment, you don't have a job either."

"Thanks for reminding me."

L'abuela says: "That a girl as qualified as you, with all her studies, after so many years of work in Barcelona, has to return to home to live with her parents . . ."

Father says: "Mumareta, do me a favor and don't fan the fire, it's all your fault anyway."

"My fault, and why is that?" l'abuela asks.

"Because you voted for them."

"And how do you know I voted for them anyway? Voting is anonymous!"

My father's a believer. He still has faith in the Spanish Socialist Workers' Party, the PSOE, despite the fact that it's no longer a socialist party, if it even was to begin with. He thinks that grandmother's "friends" are Evil, and so they go on like that for a while, provoking one another.

"Milagro!" cries l'abuela when my father mentions Aznar, Matas, or the People's Party.

"What's a miracle?"

"That we've been talking nearly an hour and you've yet to mention them by name, I was beginning to worry that something had come over you."

"Mumareta, I don't know why you have to say those kinds of things. If you and your friends want to destroy Mallorca, go right ahead."

"It's awful, that conference center they've built."

"It's just what we deserve: a mammoth of a thing to welcome everyone to the city. They'd have to tear it down. Put a bomb inside, like in Corsica. We'd have to become terrorists."

"But it must have cost a lot of money. They shouldn't have built it in the first place. Now that it's already there. . . ."

"Now that it's there, we'll have to keep paying for them to finish it and keep up its maintenance. Bombs away!"

L'abuela: "I don't know why they'd build a convention center so close to the sea. Or in Mallorca in the first place. We don't need so many people coming here. And I'm not quite sure but I thought I heard something about them wanting to bring in trash from abroad to burn here."

"Well of course, because it's a giant landfill! Sometimes it seems like you have no memory of anything at all. Every time these mafia sons-of-bitches win, they destroy our island."

"Sons-of-a-gun, huh? What a mouth on this one!"

"That's what they are. Corrupt sons-of-bitches, criminals."

"But they're against abortion," grandmother sighs.

"So what?"

"I can't vote for a party that defends the murder of innocent children."

Arguments in our house clear up like summer storms. Everything calms, there's no undertow, the air's cool and pleasant and the sky's so bright that no one would guess it had rained minutes beforehand.

Since retiring, my father has spent a lot of time scanning old family photos, photos that his his uncle took. After we had lunch, he showed me several of them while my grandmother fell asleep on the couch with her mouth wide open.

*

L'abuela lives with a parakeet that's in love with a mirror hanging in its cage, and a canary that needs its nails clipped by hand.

We've been looking at black and white photos of places that no longer exist and of children who are no longer children. In one of them l'abuela's father appears, the man who carried Franco's pack for him and the first person to own a car in Felanitx. He was a military man and would have liked to join the Calvary because he was good with horses. He was a Lieutenant Colonel and spent long periods in Africa with Franco's troops. During the Second Republic he was in the reserves and re-enlisted with the Nationalists when the war broke out. His wife, strong and not the nurturing type, who had once lived on the Almudaina port and with whom he had had many long conversations through the window when they were courting, had gone to see him a few times. She traveled alone. She would have never shed a tear for a man.

L'abuela's oldest brother was a pilot. She always talks about how he went flying over Felanitx port. She explains that he'd fly right up to the balcony to wave at her. The harbor is called Portocolom, but for us it's just the Port. My father remembers when l'abuela's older brother guided the plane through the masts of several boats lurching at bay, and afterward threw them candy on the balcony, but I don't believe him.

My father also remembers when a bolt of lightning entered through the garage and traveled through a hole in the stairs, turning into a ball of fire. It burned up the walls and went through the kitchen window. He and his siblings got so scared that they hid under the bed; on top of it all, one of my uncles peed his pants. I don't believe all of that either. The story of the lightning bolt, I mean; that my uncle pissed himself, sure.

L'abuela's older brother drove much like he flew and died in a motorcycle accident. During the war, the Nationalists suspected that the Republicans would attack from the sea, and expected they'd dock in Portocolom. And then something occurred to them: at night, the few people who owned vehicles would drive out to the lighthouse with their headlights on. Afterward they would make their way back with the headlights off only to return once more with the lights shining bright in an infinite procession. That way it seemed—from the sea—that they were many.

The Republicans landed at Porto Cristo.

El tio Joan had a Fiat. The few people who owned cars in Felanitx had to take the others to the warfront at Manacor. The frontlines frightened el tio Tomeu, Joan's brother-in-law, and so he offered to accompany him on those trips instead. On the ride there he'd stand on the door railing so that no one would complain about him taking up a free seat; on the way back, he'd sit next to el tio Joan, who drove. During one of the trips to Manacor, a plane passed right over their heads. El tio Tomeu got spooked and jumped off to take cover, falling into the bushes. He found himself covered in blood and all scratched up. When he came back to Felanitx, everyone asked if he'd been wounded at war.

*

We had our coffee. I said I had to get going and kissed them both goodbye. L'abuela has sunken cheeks. She told me that, even though it's because of work-related problems, she's happy to have me back in Mallorca, she feels closer to me that way. And what good was it living among the Catalans, anyway?

And my father asked l'abuela: "Do you remember when we'd weave chairs out of twine?"

MARTA ROJALS

From *We Could Have Studied Less*

(nonfiction)

Translated by Alicia Meier

"The Language of Unicorns"

It's always worth reading the international press for some perspective on the world: the other day, for example, Spain's prestigious daily *El Mundo* reported that Belén Esteban, Spanish TV star and princess of her (own) town, hired a "community manager," who writes her tweets with deliberate misspellings to "mimic the diva's style." Here's what we're dealing with: a written medium in which writing poorly is considered "stylish," like an off-the-rack skirt, a pair of Camper boots, a jihadi's beard.

But it doesn't stop there. That same day I happened upon a tweet by Kiko Rivera—the son of singer Isabel Pantoja, by profession—calling out, in Spanish, those who correct such mistakes: "Those *imbeciles* fixate on accent marks instead of on what things actually mean." I'll just point out, so we can end this abuse, that Esteban has roughly 800,000 followers, and Rivera, close to a million. Nothing really: just a few numbers after so many letters.

What we have here is a sampling of the little catastrophes that a language like Spanish, which is practiced by five-hundred million "volunteers" and considered a single body by the Royal Spanish Academy, can bear. And even if it couldn't, no one would care; it would require too much effort. This must be linguistic normality: that a speaker with hundreds of thousands of followers may brazenly ignore the basic rules of their language, and that their mammoth of a language won't even blink. Just the opposite in our case, where taking pride in ruining Catalan could kill our tongue.

There's something curious about Catalan—it must be the only language in the world, whether in terms of speaking or writing, where excellence and, by extension, the aspiration to excellence, is ridiculed. In this sense, our own Belén Esteban or Kiko Rivera would find a most receptive audience. Catalan speakers would consider it extemporaneous, humble, and of-the-streets, rising to defend it against the attacks of the naysayers, ballbusters, and bookworms who bothered to lift a finger: "Oh, and what's it to you, you Taliban piece of shit? What does an accent even do? What about a *pronom feble*? Or a comma? Kiko and Belén aren't philologists, are they? They're ordinary people!"

This is the weakness of Catalan: that even its speakers consider it second-rate. Our tolerance for being corrected is minimal—we're thankful people even speak it!—and we defend our "style" to death because, as Master Kiko would say, what matters is what it says, not how it's said. And I'm also at fault: my saint of an editor can attest to this.

This is the country where a restaurant menu not littered with errors is a Darwinian rarity. Here we will gladly hang a sign that reads "30% de desconte," as opposed to *descompte*—in the end, it's understood—but it'd always appear inconceivable to write "30% de desqüento" rather than *descuento*, or "30% of," before running to our cousin from Albacete or our daughter in London—or to the dictionary!—to avoid the ridiculous. In a climate of immediacy, proofreaders and linguistic advisers (whatever the situation may be) seem to have become a luxury, and luxuries are unwelcome in times of distress. The consequence is that, in common usage, we are denied practical contact with excellence and, therefore, the opportunity to verify that the Catalan language they taught us in school is real, not an invention, and not the language of unicorns. On the other hand, in treating it poorly, we leave significance behind.

"Springs"

In the city of more than a million and a half inhabitants, spring is a domesticated, pruned, penned-in season. A green area is an asphalt rectangle, a covered box. A green spot is a repository of toxic wastes and odorous oils. A green light is the rev of a motor, an accelerating step, the running in unison run. The trees reach out to breathe through concrete cracks in the sidewalks.

In the city of more than a million and a half, *etcetera*, municipal spring has doors, hours, a website. The passers-through wear sunglasses, stroll swept paths, take in the green from a bench between two trash bins. Children with all their vaccines in order go on outings holding hands: this is a pine leaf, this is a bush, do not walk on the lawn, stay close to the group. An excursion, an essay.

In the city of more than a million, *etcetera*, in a gridded neighborhood, on a four-lane street, on a commercial sidewalk, another tree box: at the base of a linden, a mini-spring emerges. Petals awaken, rose and lilac, floating on green clouds. A handwritten sign reads: *Thank you for letting me live here*, and you think, thank you for what? This street is not mine. Now you see it: a few squatting flowers ask permission to be.

In the city of etcetera, on an Easter Monday, overvalued lots await their moment. On Google Earth, between grey and grey, patches of sunlight. The building does not arrive and, while it does not arrive, the earth is alive and resurrected: a pinch of white, a pinch of yellow, scrappy bushes, strokes of luck. At the base of the dead cranes, a small gust of wind: wild plants and rigid stalks tickling the steel.

In the city, between the cobblestones, an abandoned pilon is mowed down beneath footsteps. One hundred thousand soles of shoes and nobody sees it. Rain falls, sand sweeps in, and a seed grasps onto it, and one day the sun commences. A hole, an outbreak, sheltered by a tiny, rusty fence. A miracle? No: an English garden. A tiny garden, circular and secret. A moment, a thought: may that tiny fence protect it for a long time.

"Civilization"

At seven in the morning, the city is really two: one for those raising their blinds, and the other for those lowering them. The birds don't sing the same way for those just coming home, their eyes lowered, as they do for those leaving and looking ahead. You can tell for the first time ever. Dawn on the streets is like a scene out of *Typescript of the Second Origin*, in which you're the only one left on Earth: everything is yours, there's everything to do, and time for everything. So, then, you take your time on the way to the sea, which must of course also be different from the other sea, the one left behind. *El mar* and *la mar*, in gender-neutral language, with their boats, *barcos*, and boats, *barques*, their fish, *peixos*, and fish, *peixes*, their monsters masculine and feminine alike. The sand, at seven in the morning, has not yet been spoiled by vulgarities. You sit on the seawall, then, awaiting.

On either side of the sun's reflection the water is cold like the arctic, the kind of sea from which pasty retirees emerge and whisper to the camera with one finger in the air: all these years, every single day, come rain or shine! And it sends shivers down your spine. If the sea is still harsh on your skin, there must be a reason. Everybody knows from the pictures, from the postcards: on a beach, three's a crowd. So, you sit on the seawall: one more figure on the sand would ruin the photo. Animals don't count.

Two dogs delight in the waves, breaking low like a breath. They meet, let you see them nipping, their upright tails wagging like metronomes. One owner chats with the other, three meters between them, as they make technical and veterinary assessments. Happy dogs are like happy children, the innocence of the world, blah, blah, blah. You automatically think about explosions, khaki uniforms, black waters, rivers of dust. Men and women like you, ragged, screaming their dogs' names amongst the rubble. And almost at the same time you return to the sea, *el mar, la mar*. To the two dogs that now frolic under the arc of a tennis ball that, ah!, doesn't touch the water. The owners egg them on with shouts and laughter, and you realize you're laughing, too. Happy dogs, like peaceful mornings and April seas, are the measure of civilization.

BEL OLID

"Nothing Will Have Taken Place but the Place"

(fiction)

Translated by Bethan Cunningham

The street has changed again. I go outside and find that, once more, the little shop on the corner isn't the little shop on the corner anymore. That everyone looks foreign, which leads me to suspect that I'm the foreign one.

Just for my own amusement, and maybe also to distract myself from my impending madness, I ask a six-foot, blonde, female passerby for the time, and she stops for a moment. And I do it in Catalan, knowing she doesn't speak Catalan, for the simple, immature pleasure of watching her think for a second before telling me she doesn't understand in a kind of German I can't situate.

I even let myself get excited for a minute and hope she's from Zurich. I've never been to Zurich and I'd love to be there right now, to have ended up there via this kind of time or space machine that my life has been lately.

But I put my hand in my pocket and retrieve three euros fifty. No Swiss francs, so I must be in the EU. For now, I'll have to resign myself to not seeing any lakes or flower sellers in squares or anything else I've always imagined Zurich must have and that, for now, I won't take in.

I must admit, at the start it was hard not to go mad, even though the first few times were simpler. I can remember perfectly the stupefying realization that I'd gone to bed at home in Barcelona and woken up, unknowingly, in Mataró: not even twenty-five miles away, just half an hour on the train, tracing, with a finger on the window, the curve of the coast and the occasional port. But, even so, it was such a forceful jolt to the laws of nature that I considered anything and everything.

I imagined a non-existent drinking session, a pill hidden in a gin and tonic that I didn't drink, a joke in poor taste from the friend who didn't bring me home.

But nothing would rid me of the irrefutable weight of having woken up at home, of having smelled my soap in the shower, of having found the coffee and sugar and *magdalenes* without thinking about it, in their place, in the yellow kitchen cupboard. Quite simply, when I went down the stairs and out into the street, there was no old man with a white moustache and Lleida accent in the little shop on the corner, and the traffic lights had moved, and the twenty-five steps to the metro stop were futile, as there was now no giant M, or steps, or elevator.

Now I barely bat an eyelid when, more and more often, I leave the house and find myself far away. I have a second breakfast in front of a newspaper that gives me clues as to where I am. I find the airport, or the train or bus station and I pay for a ticket with money that I didn't put in my pocket.

But that first time, walking disoriented towards the beach looking for the station, all of it fazed me. A while later, when I arrived at my front door, I felt afraid of opening it and not finding everything in its place. And for weeks afterward, I panicked that I might go out into the street and find a different landscape of unknown spots and unfamiliar smells. But no, nothing, nothing at all, days and days with the same buildings of the same colors.

In the end, it seems everything is overwhelmed by the sheer weight of everyday life: working at the computer, Sunday lunch at your intimidating auntie's house, buying broccoli and toilet paper and socks. Routine comes to the rescue once again. And even the most incomprehensible situation becomes shrouded in a dreamlike, hallucinatory cloud, like a fantasy so obscene that it must be relegated right to the back of the mind, like a thought left unshared because it would worry everyone.

Until, one day, after months of going out every day at ten to buy a newspaper after tending to various agencies' and editors' emergencies, I once again found myself elsewhere in the world. The second time, pointlessly, it occurred to me to turn around and climb back up the stairs to the door that bore my name. Then came that cold sweat when I saw that the stairs were no longer my stairs and that the name on flat number 2 on the first floor was not my name. I went back down and, shrugging my shoulders, faced up to the fact that this bridge rang a bell, that I'd had breakfast in this café before, that I was in Girona, which was lucky, as I knew where the train station was and it wasn't too far away, so at least I wasn't dying with fear. There are little pleasures to be found within the most absurd absurdity of the most ludicrous moments ever experienced.

With every new journey, I'm slowly feeling more and more of a sense of resignation. I've learned to be surprised by the calm flatness of Amsterdam, the striking light of Naples, the freezing rain of Glasgow, the dazzling cold of Paris. I've seen capital cities and remote villages. Now I'm not in as much of a rush to go home. I amuse myself in museums or go for a walk in the countryside. I wait patiently for trains and planes. I buy books and read them in the park. Suddenly my life of language schools and satellite TV makes sense; it becomes obvious why I chose a career in translation. In quiet periods, when all the editors are in Bologna or the agencies forget I'm here, I study Russian and read travel guides about Japan. For now, the only noticeable pattern is that I appear farther away from my world every time; I make more connections on my journey home every time.

Today, before getting in a taxi to go to the airport, I enter a quiet café and pick a table at random, next to the window, in the pale sun of early summer, opposite a man who is stirring his coffee and then, in order to look at me, raises his eyes from a guide that says "Köln" in yellow letters. I must be in Cologne, then. Or maybe not: maybe he's a Berliner planning a trip to the south. I don't know. I don't know anything anymore, and I don't care. Like I don't care about the waitress's face like a slapped ass, which makes the man's lips seem even sweeter, her unnecessarily bitter voice when she asks if I want to order, which makes his gaze even sweeter, her obvious bad mood when she slams my tea down in front of me, which makes his gait even sweeter when he gets up and comes towards me and asks, in an obviously Irish brand of English, if I mind if he sits next to me.

And he looks at me with a shadow as deep and dark as my own, with such deep doubt invading every wrinkle on his forehead that I don't need to ask where we are to know that he's lost too, that he can't get his bearings from his guide, that, like I've done so many times before, he's trying to find himself, to take refuge in the perpendicular peace of streets on maps, of spaces with names that mean something, with names you can repeat to strangers so that they nod and smile and tell you where you're going or where you're coming from, if you're lucky.

So yes, he looks at me. And the shadow swallows me up and frightens me and shakes me, and all I can do is leave before he opens his mouth, before he tells me his story, which is as unclear and inexplicable as my own. And I flee from sharing this irrationality that, until now, was bearable just because it was my own, exclusive, latent. Because it didn't happen to anyone else. Because, if you don't talk about it, the incomprehensible simply doesn't exist.

I get up and fly off through deserted streets, fly with my hair in the wind. I run aimlessly, run without hearing cars or birds, run until I'm breathless, and even when breathless I keep running. And I finally stop, at the front door on a street that's the same street, that's my street this time. Surprisingly, I climb the same old steps and find them cold, and read a name on the door that I know is my own but seems alien to me. I'm scared it will be in finding myself that I lose myself.

But I stick my hand in my pocket and find keys that fit in the lock effortlessly, as though five minutes ago I was actually in a café in Eixample and not in some neighborhood in some corner of Germany opposite an Irishman, as though home had never moved from its place, as though I'd made all this up.

And the most worrying thing is that it's easy for me to accept this, to open the door, go to the kitchen, make coffee. And sit next to the window and wait for the bell to ring and for it to be him, to invite him in and to spend the day telling each other about impossible journeys to unspecific countries. To liberate tears with words, fear with caresses, helplessness with gestures. To erase the irrationality of life with the irrationality of pleasure.

And there's that vertigo again when, in the morning, in front of the unmade bed, I'm not sure whether I'm at my house or his.

Authors, Editors, Translators, Visual Artist

Jennifer Arnold
Jennifer Arnold is a research fellow at the University of Birmingham. She is compiling and translating a critical anthology of Spanish and Catalan exile literature as part of the Leverhulme-funded project Inner and outer exile in fascist Germany and Spain: a comparative study. She was awarded her PhD in 2017 and her thesis examined the translation and reception of Catalan literature into English. She translates professionally from Spanish and Catalan, specializing in academic and literary texts. Jennifer was the recipient of the Emerging Translator Mentorship for Catalan in 2016, organized by the Writers Centre Norwich, UK, during which she spent a year working with Peter Bush, translating the collection of short stories *El parèntesi més llarg* by Tina Vallès.

Mònica Batet
Born in Tarragona (Catalonia), Mònica Batet studied Catalan Philology at the Universitat Rovira i Virgili. She has written four novels and several short stories. Her second novel (2012), *No et miris el Riu (Don't Look at the River)*, was selected as a finalist for the Crexells award. Her third novel (2015), *Neu, óssos blancs i alguns homes més valents que els altres (Snow, Bears and Some Men Braver than Others)*, received a subsidy from the Institució de les Lletres Catalanes.

Megan Berkobien
Megan Berkobien is an activist, writer, and translator. She is currently pursuing her PhD at the University of Michigan. Her work has appeared in the journals *Words without Borders*, *A Public Space*, and *Poets & Writers*, among many others. She founded the Emerging Translators Collective in 2017.

Lolita Bosch
Lolita Bosch (1970) was born in Barcelona, but has lived in Albons (Girona, Spain), the US, India, Oaxaca, and Mexico City—she has long considered Mexico her second home. She is a novelist and also writes children's and young adult fiction, pens essays, edits anthologies, researches, and works as a journalist. Her work has been recognized

with various prestigious prizes, brought to both cinema and stage, and translated into various languages (though not English). Bosch's work is both profoundly personal and experimental.

Mireia Calafell

Mireia Calafell (1980) is the author of *Poètiques del cos* (2006), *Costures* (2009) and *Tantes mudes* (2014). In 2015, she was awarded the Lletra d'Or for the best book published in Catalan for *Tantes mudes*, which has recently been translated into Spanish (Stendhal Books, 2016). Her poetry has been included in anthologies published in Argentina, Brazil, Holland, the UK, the United Arab Emirates, and Spain.

Esperança Camps

Esperança Camps is a Menorcan journalist and writer who now resides in Valencia. She is the winner of several literary prizes, including the Joanot Martorell Prize and Critics' Prize for Valencian Writers for her first published work, the City of Alzira Prize, the Odissea Readers' Prize, the Vicent Andrés Estellés Prize, and the Blai Bellver Prize. In addition to teaching creative writing at the University of Valencia, she writes short stories and novels and works as a journalist in print, radio, and television.

Harriet Cook

Funded by the London Arts and Humanities Partnership, Harriet Cook is a third-year PhD student at King's College London where she is working on medieval Galician-Portuguese love lyric. She graduated from the University of Cambridge in 2013 with a degree in Modern and Medieval Languages and has since completed an MA in medieval studies at the University of Santiago de Compostela. In her spare time she works on translations from Catalan and Galician into English.

M. Mercè Cuartiella

M. Mercè Cuartiella is a Catalan writer and dramaturg. This story is taken from her short story collection *Gent que tu coneixes* (Proa, 2015), recipient of the Premi Mercé Rodoreda for outstanding Catalan short fiction in 2014. She has published several novels, including *Germans, gairebé bessons* (Brau Edicions, 2012) which was awarded the Premi Llibreter in the category of Catalan literature in 2012 by the Gremi de Llibreters de Barcelona i Catalunya. Her most recent novel, *Flor salvat-*

ge (Editorial Empúries) was published in 2018. She resides in Figueres with her husband, Joan Manuel Soldevilla.

Bethan Cunningham
Bethan Cunningham is a Barcelona-based freelance translator from South Wales with a love of the Països Catalans. She holds an MA in Translation Studies from Cardiff University and translates literary and cultural texts from Catalan, Spanish, and French into English.

Alba Dedeu
Alba Dedeu (1984) is a writer, translator, and editor. Her first short-story collection, *Gats al Parc* (Proa, 2011) won the Mercè Rodoreda Prize as well as the Crítica Serra d'Or prize, after which she published her second short-story collection, *L'estiu no s'acaba mai* (Proa, 2012).

Nathan Douglas
Nathan Douglas (1993) grew up in rural central Illinois, where a conveniently timed identity crisis led him to reconnect with his Cuban heritage as a teenager and become a lover of the study of languages and cultures. Since studying abroad in Barcelona while an undergraduate at Illinois Wesleyan University, Nathan has felt a special tie to the Catalan language and people. While Lolita Bosch claims Mexico as her second home, Nathan has chosen to make his own in the *ciutat comtal* whenever possible. In the US, he is currently pursuing his PhD in Hispanic Literatures at Indiana University—Bloomington, where he received his MA in 2017. Nathan broadly focuses on post-Franco Iberia, with a special focus on contemporary Catalan literature and politics; other scholarly interests include questions of gender, philosophy, and trauma, particularly as these areas of studies all convalesce upon psychoanalysis. His dissertation focuses upon writings of twenty-first-century Spanish authors, many of them Catalan, that, in his view, provide a crucial fulcrum to our understandings of a broken Spanish state that continues to hold dear to its claim to national integrity vested in the signing of its post-Franco Constitution in 1978.

Najat El Hachmi
Najat El Hachmi (Morocco, 1979) is one of the most celebrated authors of her generation. She holds a degree in Arabic Studies from the Univer-

sity of Barcelona. She is the author of a personal essay on her bicultural identity, *I Am Also Catalan*, and four novels, the first of which earned her the 2008 Ramon Llull Prize, the 2009 Pirx Ulysse, and was a finalist for the 2009 Méditerranée Étranger.

Kate Good

Kate Good is a Visiting Assistant Professor of Spanish at Grinnell College, where she teaches Spanish language and literature courses. Outside of the classroom, Kate translates academic and literary work from Catalan and Spanish to English and researches nineteenth- through twenty-first-century Peninsular literature and cultural production. Her scholarship engages with representations of gender, sexuality, and ability, examining also issues of translation and national identity in the Catalan context.

María Cristina Hall

María Cristina Hall (New York, 1991) is a Mexican-American poet, translator, and editor who works for several political analysis think tanks in Mexico City. She also teaches Chicano and border literature and is an immigration activist. Former editor of *La Cigarra* and *Mexico City Lit*.

Cortney Hamilton

Cortney Hamilton is completing a PhD in Iberian and Latin American Cultures at Stanford University. Her research focuses on questions of gender and modernity at the end of empire in nineteenth-century Spain.

Gabriella Martin

Gabriella Martin is a PhD candidate in Hispanic Languages and Literatures at Washington University in St. Louis, specializing in contemporary Iberian literature and translation studies. Her translations from the Spanish have appeared in *The Brooklyn Rail in Translation* and *Asymptote*.

Laia Martinez i Lopez

Laia Martinez i Lopez is a Catalan writer, translator, and musician. Her book-length poetry collections include *L'abc de Laia Martinez i Lopez*

(Documenta Balear, 2009), *L'estiu del tonight, tonight* (El Gall Editor, 2011), *Cançó amb esgarrip i dos poemes* (Lleonard Muntaner, Editor, 2015) i *Afollada* (LaBreu edicions, 2016).

Alicia Meier

Alicia Maria Meier is a writer and translator based in Brooklyn. She earned her MFA in nonfiction writing and literary translation from Columbia University in 2015, and currently manages Global Programs for Columbia's School of the Arts—among them the Writing Program's literary translation exchange program, Word for Word. She is the recipient of a 2016 PEN/Heim Translation Fund grant for her translation from the Catalan of Marta Carnicero's *The Sky According to Google*.

Elisa Munsó

Elisa Munsó is an artist and illustrator. In 2013, she opened her gallery El Diluvio Universal in Gràcia, Barcelona.

Bel Olid

Bel Olid (Mataró, 1977) is a Catalan writer, translator, and advocate of women's and queer rights. She is president of the Association of Catalan Language Writers and her work as an author includes children's books, short stories, novels, and nonfiction (notably her pocket guide to feminism, *Feminisme de butxaca: Kit de supervivència*).

Anna Pantinat

Anna Pantinat (Barcelona, 1977) is a scenic artist and author of *Construcció de la nit* and *De sobte, un estiu* (*Suddenly a Summer*). She sings, plays keyboards and the theremin, and composes for Pentina't Lula. Her work has appeared in *Gent Normal*, *Cabaret Elèctric*, and *Revista de letras*. She also oversees, alongside Daniel Ardura, the label Repetidor Disc.

Katherine Reynolds

Katherine Reynolds is a language teacher with a fascination for minority languages. She holds a Master's in Catalan Literature and Linguistics from the Autonomous University of Barcelona and researches linguistic and cultural normalization in the Catalan media. She has been translating Catalan since 2014.

Llucia Ramis

Llucia Ramis (Palma, 1977) is a writer and a print and radio journalist who has worked in Barcelona for over two decades. Her work was recognized in 2010 with the Bartomeu Rosselló-Pòrcel Award, and that same year she won the Josep Pla Prize for her second novel. In 2013, *Time Out Barcelona* named her Creator of the Year. Her most recent book, *The Possessions*, earned her the 2018 Anagrama Prize.

Marta Rojals

Marta Rojals was born in La Palma d'Ebre (Ribera d'ebro) in Catalonia, Spain. She holds a degree in architecture from the Universitat Politècnica de Catalunya, where she majored in theory, history, and criticism. She currently works as a translator and editor and writes nonfiction for a variety of publications, including Catalan online news source, *Vilaweb*. She is the author of two novels, *Primavera, estiu, etcètera* (La Magrana, 2011) and *L'altra* (La Magrana, 2014).

Julia Sanches

Julia Sanches is a translator of Portuguese, Spanish, French, and Catalan. Her book-length translations are *Now and at the Hour of Our Death* by Susana Moreira Marques and *What Are the Blind Men Dreaming?* by Noemi Jaffe. Her shorter translations have appeared in *Suelta*, the *Washington Review*, *Asymptote*, *Two Lines*, *Granta*, *Tin House*, *Words Without Borders*, and *Revista Machado*, among others. A former literary agent, she is cofounder of the collective Cedilla & Co.

Maria Pilar Senpau

Maria Pilar Senpau Jove is best known for her work as a dietitian and has written numerous books on topics related to food and health. This short story comes from her first work of fiction, *Gent que plora en silenci* (*Those Who Cry in Silence*) (Proa 2014).

Scott Shanahan

Scott Shanahan is a translator of Iberian languages.

Natasha Tanna

Natasha Tanna is Lecturer in Spanish at Christ's College, University of Cambridge. She specializes in modern Latin American, Spanish, and

Catalan literature, with a particular focus on gender, sexuality, exile, diaspora, and transnational identities. Her forthcoming book *Queer Genealogies in Transnational Barcelona* (Legenda) explores queer temporalities and alternative communities in works published from the 1960s onwards by the Catalan Maria-Mercè Marçal, Montevideo-born Cristina Peri Rossi, and Buenos Aires-born Flavia Company.

Tina Vallès
Tina Vallès is a writer, editor and translator from Barcelona. She is the author of numerous collections of short stories, novels and books for children. In 2012, she won the Mercè Rodoreda prize for her collection, *El Parèntesi més llarg* (*In Parenthesis . . .*), and her latest novel, *La memòria de l'arbre* (*The Memory of the Tree*), was recently awarded the Anagrama Prize. She is also co-founder and co-editor of *Paper de vidre*, an online journal dedicated to short stories in Catalan, featuring posts from some of the major names in Catalan literature today.

Mireia Vidal-Conte
Mireia Vidal-Conte is a poet and translator who has been published in *Poetari, Caràcters, Llavor Cultural, Núvol*, and *El Punt Avui*. She edited the anthology *Com elles, una antologia de poesia del s. XX* (Lleonard Muntaner, 2017). She has translated works by Anne Sexton, Anne Carson, and Brigitte Oleschinski, among others.

Anna Maria Villalonga
Anna Maria Villalonga is a writer, film critic, and lecturer in the Faculty of Philology at the University of Barcelona.

Adrian Nathan West
Adrian Nathan West is the author of *The Aesthetics of Degradation* and translator of more than a dozen books from Spanish, German, and Catalan. His fiction and essays have appeared in *McSweeney's*, the *London Review of Books*, the *New York Review of Books*, and many other journals in print and online.

We would like to thank all the following authors and publishers for granting their permission to publish the following works:

Batet, Mònica. "Hi va haver una guerra," from *24 contes al dia*. Barcelona: Godall Edicions, 2018. By arrangement with the author.

Bosch, Lolita. Excerpt from *Això que veus és un rostre*. Girona: Curbet Edicions, 2005. By arrangement with the author.

Calafell, Mireia. Selected poetry. By arrangement with the author.

Camps, Esperança. "Els ocells." By arrangement with the author.

Cuartiella, M. Mercè. "La Conxita i la senyora Concepció," from *Gent que tu coneixes*. Barcelona: Proa, 2015.

Dedeu, Alba. "Porcelana," from *L'estiu no s'acaba mai*. Barcelona: Proa, 2012. By arrangement with the author.

El Hachmi, Najat. Excerpt from *Jo també sóc catalana*. Barcelona: Editorial Columna, 2004. By arrangement with the author.

Martinez i Lopez, Laia. Selected poetry from *Venus volta*. Barcelona: Lleonard Muntaner, 2018.

Olid, Bel. "Res no té lloc," from *La mala reputació*. Barcelona: Proa, 2012. By arrangement with the author.

Patinant, Anna. Selected poetry from *De sobte, un estiu*. Barcelona: labreu edicions, 2014.

Pilar Senpau, Maria. "El llibreter," from *Gent que plora en silenci*. Barcelona: Proa, 2014.

Rojals, Marta. Excerpt from *No ens calia estudiar tant*. Barcelona: València: Sembra llibres, 2015.

Ramis, Llucia. Excerpt from *Tot allò que una tarda morí amb les bicicletes*. Barcelona: labutxaca, 2013. By arrangement with the author.

Vallès, Tina. "Taxi," from *El Parèntesi més llarg*. Barcelona: Proa, 2014.

Vidal-Conte, Mireia. Selected poetry from *Ouse*. Barcelona: labreu edicions, 2017.

Villalonga, Anna Maria. "De vegades, l'atzar," from *Elles també maten*. Barcelona: Llibres del Delicte, 2014.